How could she come on to him like that! I was getting hot under my green silk shirt. I stood there reassessing my entire relationship with Andrea. I had known her since the beginning of the school year. She had moved here from Virginia. Great. She and Seymour were both relative newcomers to town, both nostalgic for people and places left forever behind. Andrea had made friends with me right away. She was fun, and I thought she had an undercurrent of loyalty. But you never really know.

MARJORIE SHARMAT was born and raised in Portland, Maine, and now lives with her husband and children in Tucson, Arizona. She is the author of the Nate the Great series, available in Dell Yearling editions. *I Saw Him First* is her first young adult novel.

ALSO AVAILABLE IN LAUREL-LEAF BOOKS

I SAW HIM FIRST

Marjorie Sharmat

LAUREL-LEAF BOOKS

LAUREL-LEAF BOOKS bring together under a single imprint outstanding works of fiction and nonfiction particularly suitable for young adult readers, both in and out of the classroom. Charles F. Reasoner, Professor Emeritus of Children's Literature and Reading, New York University, is consultant to this series.

Published by
Dell Publishing Co., Inc.
1 Dag Hammarskjold Plaza
New York, New York 10017

This work is simultaneously published
in a hardcover edition by
Delacorte Press, New York, New York.

Laurel-Leaf Library® TM 766734,
Dell Publishing Co., Inc.

ISBN: 0-440-94009-5

RL: 5.2

Book Club Edition

Printed in the United States of America
First Laurel-Leaf printing—April 1983
Eighth Laurel-Leaf printing—January 1985

To Mitch,
for believing in me

1

Two things about me. One boring. One imbecilic.

Boring: My name is Dana Elizabeth Small.

Imbecilic: I went bananas over Seymour Finkelstein. Not head-on, front-page-news bananas, but bananas nevertheless. It was one of those embarrassing facts that belong in diaries or do-not-open-until-one-hundred-years-after-death private accounts.

Unfortunately I didn't keep it private. I intended to, but Andrea Motts found out. Well, actually I told her. It just came out, in a hot flash, like dragon's breath.

Andrea had been my sort of best friend. My real best friend was Kim Gaynor, whom I'd known forever. But now Kim lived across the country. Jennifer Manchester, who lived next door, was my next-door friend. And there was Ingrid Silver, who usually acted like I was a good friend of hers, so maybe I was. But Andrea got really close. She introduced herself to me the first day of the school year, then she called me up, then she came over, then she called me some more and came over some more. Some kids might call her a habit, but I called her a friend.

It was a weak moment when I told Andrea how I felt about Seymour. And I've been sorry ever since. Once you've *confessed* something to someone, they've got a piece of you, and you can never get it back.

We were watching a beauty pageant on TV when it happened. It was one of those contests to name Miss Someplace that encompasses every planet, including Mars. We were giggling and having a crazy time. When the contestants were asked what their future goals were, they all wanted to be something like brain surgeons for a career and they each single-handedly wanted to bring peace to the world. Andrea got up and pretended she was talking into a mike. She solemnly announced, "For the world I want a thermonuclear war, and for myself a twelve-story office building in downtown Omaha, Nebraska. But first I want the office building so I'll have time to enjoy it."

Then we both collapsed into laughter.

"What's your future goal, miss?" she asked me. She was waiting to laugh.

"I want Seymour Finkelstein to number one notice me, number two ask me out, and number three fall madly in love with me."

"Wait! You're serious," said Andrea.

[2]

"Serious," I said.

At the time I was glad I had told someone, because I had been keeping it all hidden inside me. I hadn't told my friends or my mother or anybody. I hadn't even told my dog, Melvin.

"Tell me all about it," Andrea said, switching off the TV. "Who is Seymour Finkelstein? Tell me absolutely everything."

"Everything is nothing," I said. "Seymour's new in the city as of last month. His mother or father or both got job transfers here. They're executives or something. He's in my English class. That's where I've seen him. But he hasn't seen me, if you know what I mean. That's why it's nothing. Oh, he's handsome and sexy-looking."

"Is that all?" said Andrea. "Where's your taste?"

"I haven't even *met* him. We haven't spoken, our eyes haven't met."

"Your eyes haven't met? That sounds gloppy," said Andrea.

Andrea was always making up or rearranging words. "So what are you going to do about it?" she asked. "Trip him or something?"

"I'm going to sort of hang around after class and make eye contact and see what happens," I said.

"You mean you're going to try to pick him up?" said Andrea.

I hate her translations.

Andrea was cool about it at the time. She turned the

TV back on. She switched to a station where there was an interview with the first lady. The first lady was being asked which clothes designers are her favorites. Andrea waltzed around the room. "Ladies and gentlemen of the press," she said, "I buy all my clothes exclusively in K mart. Got that? But I've seen a few things in Woolworth's that tempt me, so I may not be *exclusive* K mart much longer. I prefer the adventure of bending over those tables where you have to shove and push to find your right size, but I do occasionally make a selection from a well-ordered rack."

I switched off the TV. "I want to talk about eye contact," I said.

"Sure," said Andrea. "What about it? I think it's here to stay."

"I want to make eye contact with Seymour Finkelstein."

"Be my guest," said Andrea.

"I mean, tell me how to *do* it."

"Well," said Andrea, "you've got eyes, right? And he's got eyes, right? So you both use them and that's it."

Andrea was about to turn the TV back on.

"Help me, Andrea. You're more experienced than I am."

"I just did. All you need are the eyes, which you have, and then you just face the other-eyes person."

"I do? What if we're going in the same direction?"

"Really, Dana. You have to face him. How can you

make eye contact if you're both going in the same direction? Okay, settled? Two pair of eyes, facing each other, and you've got it."

"Thanks, Andrea."

"Anytime."

I was a bundle of nerves the next day. I was anxious to put into action Andrea's eye-contact strategy with Seymour Finkelstein. Seymour sat a few rows in front of me in English class. I was forever staring at his shoulders. I had a weakness for broad shoulders and his were particularly horizontal. Other girls stared at him, too. Seymour was easy to fall for. You didn't have to talk yourself into it. You didn't have to enumerate his wonderful qualities. They just blasted out at you in a refined sort of way.

English class was finally over. It was time! I picked up my books and slowly walked to the door. So did Seymour. I was watching him out of the corner of my eye. I had a problem. I was definitely going in the same direction as he was. I walked faster. I rushed out of the room, turned around, and walked toward the room, hoping that if anyone noticed, they'd think I had a reason for going back to where I had just come from. My reason was heading toward me. I looked up at him. He actually looked down at me. He said, "Hello."

Seymour Finkelstein said "Hello" as if he had samples of them to give out. Still, he could have ignored me. I said "Hello" back.

Seymour walked on. I walked on. He was better off than I was. He knew where he was going. To the next class. But me, I was still walking into the class I had just come from. I took care of that problem fast. I looked under my desk as if searching for something lost. Fortunately nobody was kind enough to inquire about what I had lost. So I straightened up and left the room.

Mission, worthwhile or not, accomplished.

2

I was dying to tell Andrea what had happened, or what hadn't happened. I thought that maybe she could tell me whether anything actually had happened. But whenever I saw her that day, there were other kids around. And I knew that after school her cousins were coming to visit for the weekend. I put the *hello* incident in the back of my mind and tried to remember what I was supposed to have learned in English class. Something about contemporary authors. Could I call up Seymour and ask him what I was supposed to have learned? Or maybe I could walk on spikes, scorch my hair down to its roots, and cut my throat simultaneously.

When I got home from school, my mother was busy in the kitchen. My mother and father have what I think are interesting careers. They are hosts of a half-hour daily TV talk show called *Small Talk*. (Our last name is Small, great!) In our city they are celebrities, and some of it spills over on me. Are *you* related to the Smalls? I want my own talk show when I graduate from my present and future schools. All my extracurricular activities in high school have to do with speech, dramatics, and communication. I'm only fifteen, but I've been hanging around my parents' sets for years, and I know *everything*! I think of myself as show biz, but I don't come out and say it, because it can turn people off. I think I've made a few friends just because kids want to be friends with the daughter of celebrities, but I think I lost out on making some friends because they were jealous of my parents' show. I don't want to gain *or* lose friends that way, but that's how it is, and I accept it.

Before I had a chance to say hi to Mom and put my books down, Jennifer came by. I guess she had seen me pass her house. She came into the kitchen to talk to Mom. Jennifer *loved* Mom. Mom knew lots of fascinating people from interviewing them on the show, and Jennifer was a real fan type. But Mom wasn't that nuts about Jennifer. Jennifer once told Mom that she would never want to get involved with anyone who *sweats*. I mean, just like that. Doesn't everyone sweat? So Mom thought Jennifer was not only a snob, but peculiar.

Jennifer was also beautiful. Not modestly beautiful, but *I know I'm* beautiful.

Mom said, "I've got some notes to go over for next week's programs," and she left the kitchen. Jennifer and I were left alone.

Immediately Jennifer said to me, "I just saw that fantastic new guy who moved here last month."

"What fantastic new guy is that?" I asked, knowing full well what fantastic new guy it was. How many Seymour Finkelsteins are there?

"Well, his name is Seymour Finkelstein, but he looks like his name is Derek Revere or something."

"What's wrong with the name Seymour Finkelstein?" I asked. (I had repeated the name to myself a thousand times already. It always sounded just right.) "Have you met him?"

"No, but I saw him. Andrea pointed him out today."

Andrea? What business did she have pointing out *my* prize? She hadn't seen him as of last night, so she must have hunted him down just today. Inspired by my raving about him, no doubt. I had an uneasy feeling of something being done behind my back. "Andrea pointed him out?" I repeated.

"Well, with her eyes. I saw her staring at this hunk, and I asked who he was, and she said she didn't know, but I think she did. Anyhow, I asked Rosalie Brandon and she told me his name. Have you met him?"

"In a way," I said. I was not going to tell Jennifer about the personal, private *hello* that Seymour and I had exchanged that very morning. It was my secret.

I looked at Jennifer. I suddenly had this terrible

vision of how absolutely smashing she and Seymour would look together. It made me sick to my stomach.

Sitting next to Jennifer was not the best place to think about my own looks. My hair and eyes are brown and green respectively, and I'm not fat and I'm not thin. So far so good. But I have this washed-out look, like I'm permanently trapped under a fluorescent light. My looks are what you would call *dependent*. That is, they're dependent upon my personality. *Needy* is more like it, I guess. They need my personality in order to get by. When my personality is working, I look okay. Without it, my looks descend into limbo. Jennifer could close down her personality, and there would be her looks, glowing all by themselves. I never wanted to compete with Jennifer.

Mom came back into the room. I think she was hoping Jennifer would leave. But all Mom had to do was mention sweat or armpits or going to the bathroom or something gross like that, and Jennifer would gather up her sensibilities and beat an exit.

I guess Jennifer sensed Mom's moodiness, because she got up to leave. I never found out why she came over. But I was worried that it was to talk about Seymour Finkelstein, because we didn't really talk about anyone else.

As Jennifer closed the door behind her, Mom said, "Guess who will be a guest on our show?"

This is a common-enough question in my house, and the usual joking answer is King Kong or Superman.

But Mom was really excited this time, and she didn't wait for my answer.

"Buzz Janos!" she said. "Merely the hottest tennis player in the country. And now he's a best-selling author. God, we need him. Lately we've had a string of bores."

"How can you say that, Mom? Some people are dying to know how to earn a million dollars in twenty minutes. Or lose fifty pounds while still being able to eat seaweed. Or be reborn under a better astrological sign."

Mom sat down and faced me. "Listen, Dana. We're going to have contract troubles again at the station. The ratings go up, the ratings go down . . ."

"But *Small Talk* is very, very popular with the age groups that spread the most money around. Isn't that what counts?"

Mom shrugged. I really felt sorry for her. And for Dad. Every few years, depending upon how long their contract had to run, they had renewal worries. Would the station renew? Would their program be cut from half an hour to fifteen minutes? Would their nice 10–10:30 A.M. Monday through Friday slot be demoted to 5 A.M. Sunday mornings? All sorts of potential disasters. Mom and Dad were insecure because they both made their livings from the same source.

Mom went on. "It's all very fragile, Dana. Most people equate high-visibility jobs with money. They equate glamour with money. They equate knowing famous people with money. But you and I know that's not necessarily the way it is."

My parents always used their jobs as taking-off points for "little lessons about life," as I called their talks. But I was learning. If you have a tiny store and not many customers, people think of you as a Mom-and-Pop combo struggling for a piece of the pie, and they feel sympathetic that your business isn't better. But once you're in front of a TV camera all shiny like a star (even if it's only from sweat), they won't feel one bit sorry for you if your jobs are in jeopardy. They almost think you deserve it because you picked a career that wasn't solid.

I wasn't sure what I would do with this particular little lesson about life inasmuch as I still wanted to be a TV host.

When Dad came home, we toasted Buzz Janos' coming to town. We had a wonderful supper. No one brought up the subject of contracts. My mind had left the subject of contracts anyway. It was back to Seymour and his *hello*. I didn't want to tell my parents about him. They might have understood how I felt about Seymour, but I wanted to keep it to myself. And Andrea. Andrea? I was beginning to feel creepy about Andrea. Why had she tracked down Seymour just as soon as she could? I didn't want that to bother me, but it did.

3

After supper I went to my room and replayed and replayed in my mind Seymour's *hello* and my *hello* back. I tried to remember the inflection in his voice, if there was one. I tried to remember the expression on his face, if there was one. Then I worked on vibes, nuances, movements, posture, redness of his face, condition of his pores, possible hand tremors—anything that might tell me what he was really thinking.

For the next couple of days I did this over and over and over again. I didn't see Seymour again because it was the weekend. All I had to go on was one dumb *hello*. I was getting tired of recycling the same crumb. When I was feeling optimistic I would think about the *hello* and I was sure that Seymour liked me a lot. When I was feeling down I thought that Seymour thought I was a zero. I was using the same *hello* to come to opposite conclusions. If my parents could get as much mileage out of a crumb of food as I got out of that *hello*, they'd never have to go to the supermarket again, or worry about contracts. We'd all be nourished forever.

By the time Sunday night came around, I had exhausted all the possibilities of what Seymour's *hello* could or couldn't mean. I had also exhausted myself.

I called Andrea. I needed her.

"Have your relatives left?"

"Yes."

"Come over."

Andrea came right over. I told her about the *hello*. She looked me straight in the eye.

"You know what *hello* really means," she said. "It means *hello*. That's it. No more. No less. It's one of the most nothing words in the English language. Let's face it. All by itself, all by its lonesome, *hello* means *hello*."

"You're making me feel stupid," I said.

"It's not stupid to want something to be more than it is. Maybe that's what life is all about. I think that will be my profound statement for this year. But, Dana, you need more to go on. You're imagining, supposing, maybe hallucinating. Here's our latest hallucinogenic product, ladies and gentlemen. It's called Hello. It will transport you to regions of the mind as yet unexplored."

Andrea laughed, and so did I. She was waking me up. I was getting nowhere by mooning around. I had to move *forward*.

"I need a plan," I said.

"Now you're talking," said Andrea.

"I don't have a plan."

"Make one up. You've got lots of options."

"I have?"

"Sure," said Andrea. "You could do something daring or conservative or simple or complicated or tacky or straightforward or obnoxious or . . ."

"Hold it! What do you mean?" I asked.

"Take tacky, for example. That's taking off all your clothes in the middle of English class. That's ultimate tacky." Andrea held up her hand as if to ward me off. "Only kidding, only kidding. But I have an idea. You could give a big, big party and invite him. It would be so big that he wouldn't catch on that it was really just for him."

"My folks wouldn't let me have a big party," I said.

"Well, how about this? *Tell* him you're having a big party and invite him. Then invite a lot of kids who you think won't come. And you can be tricky. If, for instance, the debating team is going to be out of town, plan the party for when they'll be away and invite them. Then you can always mention them as kids you invited to your *big* party. So when it turns out to be a small party Seymour won't be suspicious."

"It sounds complicated," I said.

"I already told you that complicated is one of your options," said Andrea.

"What if he doesn't accept?"

"Ask him *first*," said Andrea. "If he doesn't accept, then you won't have the party at all."

"Won't he find out that he was the only person invited to a party I didn't have?"

"No, he won't go around checking. Why should he? I'm telling you this is a neat plan, Dana. And listen, it sure beats *hello*."

So it was decided.

But there was something missing from our conversation. I was waiting for Andrea to tell me she had now seen Seymour. But she didn't say a word. I gave her an opening. I mentioned his terrific looks again, thinking that would give her a chance to say, "I know. I saw him."

But Andrea said, "He must be fantastic-looking."

Suddenly I was sorrier than ever that I had confided in Andrea. But now it was too late. I had a down-in-the-pits feeling that I was going to pay a high price for her advice.

4

This is how it will go:

"Seymour, hi."

"Hi."

"I'm having a party at my house and I'm inviting you."

"Oh, God, I thought you'd never ask!"

"You mean you've been waiting for this invitation?"

"I've been waiting for *anything* from you. The flicker of an eyelash, the faintest of smiles, the tiniest of nods. *Anything!* I've been living on that *hello* you gave me, hoping that it *really* meant something."

"I didn't know. I didn't know."

"And someday, not too far into the future, I'm planning on a kiss. An actual kiss. I dream about that kiss all through English class. That's why my grades are rock-bottom and I've only been in school five weeks. Rock bottom usually takes longer."

"I know. I know."

"If I could have that kiss right now, I might do better in English."

"Right here in front of the entire class?"

"I'm not ashamed of my passion, are you?"

"It depends. Is that the same as love, Seymour? I'm a cautious person."

"I love you, Dana."

"That does it." *(Embrace. Kiss.)*

Then again, it could go this way:

"Seymour, hi."

"Whatcha want?"

"I want to invite you to a party at my house on—"

"Save the details. I'm not coming."

"Why not?"

"Because I have extrasensory perception and I know you're freaked out over me. Your vibes are boring and gross and they're wrecking my grades. That's why my grades are rock-bottom and I've only been in school five weeks. Rock bottom usually takes longer."

"I know. I know."

"I have a nickname for you."

"Will I like it?"

"Only if you like stupidjerk stupidjerk stupidjerk. And here, I have a present for you."

"Oh, you really didn't have to."

"I did have to. It's a one-way ticket to a foreign country of your choice."

"But—"

"I want you to find somebody there to annoy."

"But I'd rather annoy *you*."

"I know. I know."

"Is it possible that you love me, Seymour?"

"Is it possible that you're insane?"

There was one thing I knew as I sat in English class. I would *have* to invite Seymour right after class. I had been putting it off for a week. But I couldn't put up with another day of my own fantasies.

I did it fast. When class was over, I marched right up to Seymour Finkelstein.

"I'm having this really big party," I said, "and I was wondering if you'd like to come."

I said it much faster than I had rehearsed it. I think I ran "really" and "big" together. And I sort of swallowed "party." But it was out, after a wild, topsy-turvy week of getting up my courage, going chicken, and telling myself how fortunate Seymour Finkelstein was to exist on the very same planet as Dana Small. Waiting for the right moment is probably a great title for a song, but it's the pits in real life. Some people get old waiting for the right moment. Sometimes it never comes.

And now Seymour Finkelstein was looking down at me. My invitation was registering.

"A party?" he said. "When?"

Oh, I had forgotten something. Like the date.

"Three weeks from next Saturday, which is just about four weeks from now. A better way to remember it is the twenty-eighth."

"The twenty-eighth?"

"Yuh."

"Um."

The um didn't go with his broad shoulders. *They* looked decisive.

"Sounds great," he said finally.

"You're the most wonderful creature God ever created," I said, to myself. But I wanted to say it to him.

"Where do you live?" he asked.

Perfectly sensible question. I told him my address.

He jotted it down on a piece of paper. I was finally part of Seymour Finkelstein's official written-down life.

"What time does the party start?" he asked.

Rats, I was making him work hard! My prepared speech had included all vital information arranged in order of importance. Too bad I forgot most of it.

"Around eight," I said, "give or take a few minutes. You won't get arrested if you show up a few minutes late." Now that the business of inviting him was over, I wanted to chat. To be normal and natural and kid around. But Seymour smiled faintly, said, "Thanks," and, "See ya," and walked on.

Then he turned around and came back. "What's your name?" he asked.

My name? How could he not know my name? Ms. Tree, our English teacher, was forever calling on me. By name. Seymour's question made me feel like a flea that had alighted on him, trying to establish an unlikely relationship. How many fleas do you know by name?

"Dana Small."

"Oh, yuh, that's right. I remember." Seymour waved his hand slightly as he walked away.

Whew! It was over. And I had to sort it out. The good news. The bad news. He had accepted. That was the overwhelmingly good news. But he was kind of blah about it. "Sounds great," "Thanks," "See ya," and "What's your name?" were not causes for jubilation.

I had to get to my next class, which was fortunate. Otherwise I would have stood outside my English classroom while my optimistic side battled with my pessimistic side for supremacy.

"Terrific!" was Andrea's verdict when we got together for lunch. "He accepted!"

"I think he accepted out of shock," I said.

"Shock, schmock, who cares," said Andrea. "Only three weeks from Saturday. I can hardly wait."

"What do you mean *you* can hardly wait?" That creepy feeling I had about Andrea was there again. "He's mine, Andrea," I said. I didn't like the way I said it. My voice had the sound of spoken-for territory and faint belligerency. What was happening to me? Besides, Seymour Finkelstein *wasn't* mine.

"You mean you own him?" said Andrea. I didn't like the sound of her voice either. I once read a story about a woman falling in love with a man she had never met just by hearing wonderful things about him. Sort of continuous press releases. Was this happening to Andrea? Was I giving Seymour an irresistible build-up?

I changed the subject.

I was glad when school was over. I had an appointment to meet Mom at the TV studio. From there we were going shopping. She and Dad had given their okay to my party, "which I might or might not have," as I had described it without explaining why. I wanted a new outfit for my maybe/maybe not party. I could always use a new outfit.

I'm just about the only girl I know who would rather shop with her mother than a friend. Mom has wonderful taste. She's on TV five days a week and she wears something new each time. I don't know if she actually *has* to. In fact most viewers would probably identify better with her if they could look at her and say, "What? Wearing that same old rag again!" But that's not the way it is on TV. So Mom assembles all these bits and pieces of a wardrobe, lots of separates, and even though she might repeat what she's wearing, you don't notice because it's matched with something different. I think she owns at least 150 scarves, and the same number of convertible collars. She has different hairdos, too. She keeps them on the upper shelf of her closet. They're all brunette.

I could hardly wait to say to Mom, "The party's on."

5

Mr. Carlin had his back to me. From the back he looks like you'd never want to know him from the front.

Mr. Carlin is the owner of the TV station where my parents have their talk show. He's been there for three of the eight years my parents have had the show, and he's managed to make life as miserable as possible for them. I wanted them to switch channels, so to speak. There are four TV stations in our city, including public TV, and I thought it would be great if Mom and Dad took their show to one of them. But they hadn't had any offers.

Mr. Carlin turned around. "What, you again?"

Mr. Carlin has one good quality. He isn't a hypocrite. He's just plain nasty. That's it. He doesn't bother with smiles, charm, flattery, or even civility. I wonder what his parents were like. Were they human? Did they ever serve milk and cookies? I bet they kicked sick dogs.

Maybe Mr. Carlin would have been nicer to me if I hadn't hung around the station so much. He thought I was a nuisance. But I loved being at the station. My parents' show is aired in the morning when I'm at school, but most of the shows are taped in advance, and I've watched a lot of tapings. I've given suggestions for interviews, too. And sometimes at home I've pretended to be a guest while my parents were practicing what loomed as a particularly tough interview. I *know* I could interview on my own. I hate myself for this, but I've fantasized my parents simultaneously coming down with a very mild but thoroughly revolting-looking illness—eyes and nose running, blotchy red faces, etc.—that kept them off the air. Guess who the substitute host is.

"Hello, Mr. Carlin." I smiled. I always acted like he was a wonderful human being.

Mom was replaying a tape she had made with a visiting politician. Sometimes Mom did the interviews, sometimes Dad did the interviews, and sometimes they did joint interviews. Their contract called for their appearances to be evenly divided, but when you tuned in to the program, you usually didn't know in advance whom you were getting. Mr. Carlin once had some kind of evil plan to poll the viewers to see who was their favorite, Mom or Dad, but that was so disgusting that everyone at the station actually came out and said it stank. It made me think that if everyone at the station rose up against Mr. Carlin, he'd have to change his ways. Mr. Carlin as Mr. Nice Guy, kissing babies, licking boots . . . anything to keep the peace. It couldn't be.

Mom beckoned me in and we watched and listened to the rest of the tape together. Then we left to go shopping.

Shopping was great. Mom helped me pick out a few separates, but she left all the final decisions up to me, of course. We agreed on everything except a bright-green mandarin-style silk shirt that I loved. "The worms spin it and then they leave you with all the problems of taking care of it," she said. But I bought the shirt.

That afternoon my whole life felt up. I had a looking-forward kind of feeling. Color me rosy.

6

"How would you like to be on TV?" Dad asked at dinner.

I grinned. He knew the answer before he asked the question. Then I asked, "Doing what? What show? And why?"

"*Small Talk* is the show, and you'd be the guest."

Quickly I tried to think of something I had achieved in life. Then it came to me. "I'd go on because I'm your daughter, and nepotism, although not widely admired, is somewhat more acceptable than lust or greed or the other things that some of your guests pitch."

Dad laughed. We always kidded about his guests. "Well, in a way you're right," he said. "You would be going on because you're our daughter, but you'd be right for our program theme."

"What's the theme?"

"Well, I hesitate to call it a program about a typical teenager. Maybe a representative teenager. At any rate, we need an articulate teenager, and that's you."

"Articulate teenagers are usually boring to the rest of the population. Why do you want to do this program, anyway?"

"It's a kind of public-service program, Dana. The schools like this sort of thing. *Encourage* this sort of thing."

"Oh, I get it. It's one of those deadly programs that bore the pants off everyone who isn't involved in it. It's one of those dull, dull things that nobody watches. I'll do it."

"But, Dana, I thought you *wanted* to be seen on TV!"

"Sure," I said. "It's easy to want something when you're not faced with getting it. Could I think it over? I don't know how the kids at school would take it. It's one thing to be on TV, but another to be on your parents' show. Maybe I'll talk it over with one of my, how would you put it, contemporaries?"

I wound up talking it over with my dog, Melvin. I was self-conscious about approaching my friends. It just seemed too personal and too complex. Melvin is only programmed for tail-wagging good news and slinking, tail-between-the-legs bad news.

"See, Mel, there's going to be a TV program about a

typical teenager. Me. Some typical. I'm the daughter of the program's hosts. And it's not such a great honor to be on this program. It could be a chance to make a fool out of myself. A lot of kids would pass that up. So whatcha think, Mel?"

Melvin wagged his tail optimistically. A clear go-ahead answer. Melvin usually wags his tail, so I was cheating.

It was decided to tape the show at home. Good. I would certainly feel more at home at home. I'm sure that's what my parents had in mind. I had fantasized about being the perfect host, but I'd never dreamed of being the guest. Suddenly I felt a little nervous.

We taped one evening. A small crew showed up from the station and set up lights and cameras. They were cheerful and friendly. We all knew one another, of course. Melvin sniffed everyone, hung around for a while, and then went back to the kitchen.

My parents were fidgeting. I guess they figured I could bring down the House of Small all by my lonesome. I was wearing a big, long-sleeved shirt and long pants, both of which I hoped could hide body tremors. We had gone over and over what they were going to ask me, but I felt totally blank just when we were ready for the taping.

First, Mom introduced me as her daughter, Dana. But it sounded to me like she said "Danish," and I found out later, in the replay, that she did. But they kept it in because they figured no one would notice.

Mom wanted so badly for it to go right for me. Dad forgot that he wasn't wearing a necktie, and he was busy adjusting it. Off to a roaring start.

Mom turned toward me. "Dana, I'll start right off with a nuts-and-bolts question. What does it feel like to be a sophomore in high school?" I thought Mom would start off with a better question.

"Well, Mom, it's complicated. All kinds of things are coming at you at the same time. Intellectual, emotional, physical."

Mom nodded sympathetically. She was used to platitudes. She was also used to pitches and rehearsed speeches that sound unrehearsed. She was used to soul baring and occasional body baring. She was used to the icky and the gushy and the repulsive. Mom was vomit-proof.

"Then again," I added, "this all sounds like a platitude."

Mom's eyes widened in horror.

Dad's hands became busier than ever at his neck.

The comments I had so carefully prepared in advance turned over and died. I was now winging it.

"I'm only one person," I said. "I can tell you about a typical day in my life, and maybe you can relate it to what other kids do and feel. Although possibly . . ."

"*Tell* us," said my mother. I think it was a plea.

So I told them about a typical day. With no mind-boggling perceptions, no insights, and no mention of Seymour Finkelstein, although that would have livened things up. I was the kind of guest Mom calls "a nonprescription sleeping pill."

Dad, in an attempt at resuscitation, asked me what teenagers do for fun and recreation.

I wished he hadn't asked. My answer would not only not resuscitate the show, it might demolish it. Dad really wouldn't want to know what some teenagers do for fun and recreation.

"Well, Dad, *I* listen to records and go to parties and read and swim and . . ."

I was left with a hanging *and*, so Dad neatly finished up by saying, "And watch television."

Dad had broken one of his own rules, which was never to complete a guest's sentence.

I said, "Well, yes, I do watch TV. But most television is for noodleheads. In fact, the only show I watch on this channel is yours."

It was an awful moment. The words were out before I knew they were coming. I could visualize Mr. Carlin calling a hit man to take care of me.

At that point Mom and Dad decided it would be appropriate and also program saving for them to talk about the life of the *parents* of a typical teenager.

They were fantastic. They talked to each other, joked with each other just as if they were sitting in their own living room, which of course they were. I knew they were also desperately trying to figure out how to get me and the teen point of view back into focus.

Just then a tail went by. Melvin came bounding into the room and jumped onto my lap. "A typical teenager's dog," I murmured, trying hard to keep the program's theme.

Melvin really saved the day. You could tell the crew was happy, as well as relieved, that he showed up. They were grinning all over the place.

"Another member of the household," Dad said, once again trying to adjust his tie. Melvin licked Dad, which helped a lot under the circumstances. We were beginning to look like the kind of wonderfully wholesome American family that turns your stomach.

I couldn't believe it when the time was up. It had felt like a life sentence. Somewhere in the program I think I stopped using my personality, and you know what happens to my face when I do that. I'm sure I looked ugly.

The star of the show was indisputably Melvin, but nobody came right out and said so.

Two days later I saw the tape played at the studio. I picked a time when I knew Mr. Carlin wouldn't be there. Mom and Dad were pleased, except for the Danish and the tie and the platitude and the television remark. They said that the television remark would be edited out. Mr. Carlin had exploded when he had heard what I said. I didn't notice what I was saying on the tape because I was concentrating on a zit that the camera had discovered for me. Discovered, magnified, and made a star of.

I was now determined to tell absolutely no one at school about the show. I have to admit I was disappointed. Being a guest isn't for me. I know I'd be better as host. The show was going to run during school hours, so I wasn't worried that kids would see it.

But the next day mimeographed fliers went all over school announcing the upcoming TV program about a typical teenager, "our own" Dana Small. The assembly committee was arranging to have TV sets in the gym and the auditorium.

Andrea came up to me. "What a thrill," she said. "Between this and your party, Seymour will notice you!"

Seymour! He had never noticed me in person. Now he would carry around the image of how I looked on TV. He might become the permanent mental custodian of my zit.

The show was scheduled to be aired two days later. Mom and Dad said I could not get violently ill. They said the show was charming. Everything had been edited perfectly.

I was supposed to watch the setup in the auditorium. Me and dozens of other kids. It was a big-screen TV. Ever seen a multimagnified zit?

Two minutes before the showing I went to the bathroom. Two minutes after the showing I left the bathroom. I don't even know if I was missed. When I got back to the auditorium I got congratulations all around. It didn't mean anything. It was just politeness.

But Seymour Finkelstein came up to me at lunch and said I was terrific. It was the first time he had spoken to me since I had invited him to the party. He sounded *sincere*!

At home I thought about that. I was terrific when I thought I wasn't? I cannot figure things out.

7

"You were great," said Jennifer.

We were sitting in my kitchen. My mother hadn't left the room this time. She was interested in what Jennifer was saying about the program. Maybe she was warming up to Jennifer.

"I think that people *relate* to you and your husband, Mrs. Small."

"Really?"

"Yuh. Like people don't relate to me. I mean, as much as they relate to you, that's how much they don't relate to me."

"What do you mean, Jennifer?" Mom was curious.

"Well, I'm spectacular-looking, right?"

Mom's jaw dropped. Mine followed.

"I'm not supposed to say that, am I? It's not modest or acceptable, is it? But see, I have to face the way I look and go on from there."

"You do?" asked Mom, jaw still dropped.

"Where do you go?" I asked. Wherever it was, I was sure I'd like to go, too.

"Are you making fun of me?" Jennifer asked.

I didn't know if we were or weren't. I honestly didn't.

"I'll admit it's no burden to be beautiful," said Jennifer. "It's really a gift I'd never return, okay?"

Mom and I felt we had to say okay. We were being pulled along.

"Okay, so now I have this gift, which I really like. But I get judged by it. I'm conspicuous. That's what I am, conspicuous."

"Is that a problem?" This from Mom.

"Well, do you really *care* for conspicuous people? I don't blend. I don't fit. I'm a curiosity."

"You're normal to me. You're my friend," I said.

"That's because I'm convenient," said Jennifer. "And sometimes don't you really wish I'd grow a mole or something?"

Sometimes I really wished she would.

I had never heard such an honest revelation. Jennifer wasn't a snob. She was a realist. She was not deceived nor deluded. Somewhere, in the whole spectrum of what a friendship should mean, could mean, Jennifer knew she was losing.

I think my mother gained respect for her. I know I did.

That's why what happened at school the next day

seemed so gross. In the middle of the cafeteria Andrea started a fight with Jennifer. I wasn't there when it began, but by the time I came along, Andrea was shouting and Jennifer was trying hard not to sweat.

"You're conceited," said Andrea, "and you think everyone is going to bow down to you, that's what you think!"

"No, I don't," said Jennifer.

Kids had gathered around, half pretending to mind their own business, half trying not to miss a word. It was easy not to miss a word. Andrea was still shouting. "Conceited and spoiled rotten!" she said.

Jennifer's face was flushed. "Tomorrow you'll feel sorry you said that," she said sadly. And she walked away. She was crying.

Andrea's face was full of spite. "No, I won't!" she yelled after Jennifer.

"What was that all about?" I asked Andrea when she had calmed down. I had almost gone after Jennifer, but she had run out and I decided to let her be alone.

"Oh, it's that spoiled brat Jennifer," said Andrea.

"I heard that part already," I said. "What did she do?"

"Do? She wiggled her way up to the front of the line for dessert."

"Are you sure?" I asked. Jennifer wasn't pushy.

"Well, first she was in back, and suddenly she was in front. Right in front of me."

"So what did she say?"

"She said that Mark had been saving her place, and Mark said yes he had, but I don't care. Looks shouldn't buy you everything."

I felt wiped out by Andrea's hostility. Andrea was fun and Andrea was kooky, but underneath it all was this hard core of determination. Of wanting, of getting. Of taking care of Andrea. I wondered if there was a lot about Andrea that I didn't know. And maybe didn't want to find out. I decided to call Jennifer that night to see if she felt better.

8

I had totally forgotten that Buzz Janos was coming to town. Mom and Dad mentioned him now and then, but he left my mind in order to make room for more important things. Like my party. It was drawing closer and it was the focus of my life. Until the night Buzz Janos showed up at our house.

Buzz is a star. (Not a freako one-shot like Melvin, who received several fan letters after his TV appearance, but a *star*!) He's not only a tennis champ, he also wrote a sports book, *Tennis with Buzz*. The book really took off. That made him a double star. A tennis champ *and* an author.

Mom and Dad liked about half, or maybe less than half, of the people they interviewed on their show. They met more phonies than most people meet in a lifetime, and a whole bunch of lucky no-talents, and some truly talented, truly obnoxious people. They had heard good things about Buzz Janos. He was only twenty-one and shy, but with good TV presence. Presence is an odd word. I guess you need it to be a success on TV. I personally think that vulnerability is better than presence, because even if you look like you've got it all together, you should also look as if it could come apart at any time. Viewers identify with that.

I was a little uptight about meeting Buzz, because it occurred to me that, after all, he was a gorgeous guy, and I get that way when I meet new guys. Not to mention famous new guys that everyone wants to meet. Buzz arrived with his agent and another man who seemed to be his agent's agent or something. Mom and Dad and Buzz and the agents were huddled together talking about the show when I came into the room. Everyone looked up. I noticed that Buzz *really* looked up. "Hello," he said. It was not a crumb of a *hello*, like Seymour's. This one was solid, and right away I thought he liked me. I know I liked him. I figured he was glad to see someone near his age.

"Come join us, Dana," Dad said, but I could tell he wasn't thrilled. I knew I had interrupted something very important. I felt like a commercial for a product you never want to try that's spaced between two extremely interesting episodes of a program. Buzz was just in town for the night, and that's why everything was so intense. He planned to return sometime during the next month for three days of appearances—an autographing, newspaper interviews, and of course *Small Talk*, which would be his blast-off appearance. Everything had to be coordinated. I couldn't believe his schedule. He was going to make appearances all around the state, crisscrossing back and forth. It seemed to me that since he was already in town, he should just stay and do his stuff and then move on. But no, the timing was wrong for that. It all seemed to be figured out scientifically.

Well, I excused myself so they could get on with their planning. Buzz said, "It was nice meeting you. I'll see you again." I almost forgot about Seymour Finkelstein. I felt disloyal thinking about how nice-looking Buzz was. He looked more weathered than Seymour, older, and toothier. I went back up to my room. After all, Buzz was just a passing-through-my-life-quickly kind of guy, while Seymour could be forever. And my party was just ten days away. I started to fantasize about it.

First, although this means absolutely nothing to *me*, Seymour would be turned on by my actually getting a great party together, and being a terrific hostess.

And he would be impressed by all the friends I have. Even the ones I knew well enough to invite but who fortunately didn't accept. He would get this entire background about me. He already knew that my parents were TV stars and that I had been a guest on their program, and had been "terrific," in his sincere opinion.

Then I asked myself why I should worry about impressing Seymour. Maybe he should worry about impressing *me*. What did I really know about him? Broad shoulders do not an entire person make.

"Dana?"

Dad was calling me.

I went to the head of the stairs. "Yes, Dad?"

"Good, you're still dressed," he said, looking up. "Come join us. We're through with all of our business talk."

I went downstairs. Seymour wouldn't mind me gazing at Buzz.

When I got downstairs it looked like a little party was going on. All kinds of drinks, crackers, chips, peanuts—and everyone was laughing.

I stood there. I noticed an empty space beside Dad on the sofa, so I sat down. Buzz was sitting in the chair just off at an angle to the sofa. He started to talk to me.

"Doing your homework up there?" he asked.

"Uh, no. I was daydreaming."

Why did I say that!

"That's a great answer." He laughed. "I'm an inveterate daydreamer myself."

"What do *you* have to dream about?" I asked. "I mean, your dreams have all come true, haven't they? What's left?"

Everyone was looking at me, but Buzz was *staring*.

"Well, it's normal to yearn for something you haven't yet accomplished," he said. "To have some new goal, something to look forward to."

"Yeah, I know. My dog Melvin's got that figured out already. He always saves some of his food to eat the next day."

Everyone roared. Was my remark dumb or witty or what? I knew that my parents wouldn't laugh *at* me, and somehow I felt that Buzz wouldn't either.

Buzz. My mind raced. I was dying to know all about his life. How it felt to be a celebrity tennis star and a celebrity author and how things changed. I didn't want to zonk him with all kinds of questions, because I knew that people were always doing that to him. So I tried to ask simple, sort of quiet questions. I didn't want to pry.

And he gave me simple, quiet answers. I forgot about his overwhelming teeth.

We were all there until one o'clock in the morning. Everyone was astonished when Mom pointed out what time it was. Everyone had to get up early the next morning, including me. So our little party broke up.

As he was leaving, Buzz took my hand. He smiled and said, "I'll see you soon." It sounded personal. I couldn't stand it, it sounded so personal.

At three o'clock in the morning—who can fall asleep after so much excitement?—I thought about how great the little party downstairs had been. My party loomed as something overplanned and maybe just a plain old flop. I thought about making things happen and letting things happen. There was a big difference.

9

I was very careful about my party invitations—whom I invited and when I invited. I waited until the week before the party to invite some kids, hoping that they had already made other plans for the party night. I managed to achieve a lot of turndowns. Every time someone said no, I told Andrea and we hugged and squealed together. Mom and Dad had limited the number of my guests to "between fifteen and twenty." They were worried about damage to the house and to their budget. I invited everyone I planned to invite, including the entire debating team. I didn't really know anybody on the team very well (even though I had once planned to join to help my powers of communication). It didn't matter whether they knew me or not, because—surprise surprise—they had a match scheduled for a school one hundred miles away that weekend. I hoped it wouldn't get canceled! The team did things in unison. I couldn't imagine the entire team showing up at my house. Andrea was in stitches over the possibility.

Actually Andrea was on a big high about the party. She bought something new to wear, although she didn't come right out and tell me. She was really a pal to make *my* party seem so important. And yet I had a sense of her moving in on my life, of shifting currents or something. And she was forever talking about Seymour Finkelstein. She *still* pretended that she had never seen him. "I'm so *curious* to meet him," she said. "I always was a curious person, you know." That last bit of unsolicited explanation added to my suspicions.

And then, of course, there was Jennifer. I *had* to invite Jennifer. Jennifer, bless her beautiful curly red hair, bless her glorious figure, bless her crammed-full appointment book—Jennifer had a date for that night. Her date was taking her to a concert. *Maybe* they could drop in on my party afterward, she said, but I shouldn't count on it. I won't, Jennifer.

And what was happening with the guest of honor who didn't know he was? Absolutely nothing had happened with Seymour and me since the time he complimented me about the TV show. We did have a continuing nodding and *hi* acquaintance. After all my trouble with *hello*, I refused to attach any significance to nods and *hi's*. After all, I *had* invited him to a party.

[46]

It was only proper that he should acknowledge that I was alive. I was almost glad that he didn't come up to me, because I was afraid that he'd say he had changed his mind about coming to my party. I hoped he wouldn't get an urge to join the debating team.

10

Andrea kept insisting that it would be fun to walk by Seymour's house. We had, of course, already looked him up in the telephone book. He wasn't there. But Information had his last name listed under new numbers. And if you're tricky with Information, you can get addresses, too. We did.

"Why should I walk by his house when he's coming to *my* house?" I said. "A little restraint, Andrea!"

"Restraint! Your party is a week away. Meanwhile, you're aging."

"Aging? Are you nuts?"

"Time's going by. Time's a friend. Time's an enemy."

"We're talking next week, Andrea. Why can't I wait until next week?"

"Because this is this week. You're wasting it."

"You're really anxious about this, aren't you?" I said.

Andrea suddenly backed off. "Well, if you really don't want to."

Andrea was definitely more into this Seymour business than she was letting on.

"I'm not sure," I said. "I have to think about what I might gain and what I might lose."

"What you'll gain," said Andrea, "is running into Seymour when he's sort of free and available. You know, not at school, not in a rush. He might have hours to kill. You could kill them with him."

"What if he just says hi, and that's it?"

"What have you lost?" Andrea asked, reasonably enough.

"All right. That takes care of what I might gain. What *could* I lose?"

"Nothing," said Andrea. "That's what I'm trying to tell you. The worst thing that will happen is that you won't run into him, that's all. And meanwhile, we'll have had a nice walk."

"Of three miles each way," I said.

But I started to walk with Andrea. I still wasn't sure I wanted to head for Seymour's house, but after the first two miles it seemed to be as much destiny as destination. I seemed to be pulled there. After a long, long walk we reached Seymour's street. It was short and a dead end.

"Great," I said. "A nice, cozy dead-end street. What if Seymour asks why we're on this dead-end street three miles from my house?"

"Say something vague about being out for a stroll.

Boys aren't into details as much as girls are. It will just fly right over his head."

Seymour's house number was eight. Even that sounded private.

"There's eight!" whispered Andrea, pointing to a white-shingled house near the dead end. Seymour's house had a big "8" painted on, of all things, a plaque of a horse.

Someone was bent over a car, washing it in the driveway. The person was partially hidden, but there was a good view of his rear and his feet.

"Oh, lucky day!" said Andrea. "He's outside."

"I want to go home," I said. "This is so obvious, it screams. If a guy is too dumb to catch on to this, then I don't want anything to do with a guy that dumb."

I turned back. How good I was going to feel when I was safely off this street. My pride would be intact, and my common sense wouldn't have undergone mutation.

But Andrea had walked ahead. Straight up to Seymour's house. Stupid!!! Now what could *I* do? Wait? Follow her? Escape? I could see from my distance that Andrea was already in conversation with the car washer. The conversation was not brief. They must have had something to talk about. I was getting jealous. I walked up to Number Eight. When I got closer, I could see that Andrea was talking to a middle-aged man. It must be Seymour's father. What in the world was Andrea *doing*?

"Oh, Dana," she called when she saw me approaching. "Come here and meet this nice man who's been helping me with my directions. Do you know we're only five streets away from where we're supposed to be?"

"Yes," said the man. "And I hope your choir rehearsal hasn't started without you."

Our *choir rehearsal*? This was unreal.

"They won't start without us," Andrea assured the man. "Oh, here I am chatting away and I haven't introduced myself. I'm Andrea and this is my friend, Dana."

"I'm Millard Finkelstein," said the man.

"You seem to know the neighborhood quite well, Mr. Finkelstein," said Andrea. "Have you lived here long?"

What was she *doing*?

"As a matter of fact I'm fairly new to the city," said Mr. Finkelstein. "I'm an engineer and I got transferred here. I like it here, and my family is getting adjusted. Say, perhaps you know my older son. You girls must be about his age. He's a sophomore at Deering High School. Seymour Finkelstein."

"The name rings a bell," said Andrea. "But not very loudly. Do you know Seymour, Dana?"

A right cross to the jaw for Andrea would just about be appropriate for the occasion, I decided.

"Well, yuh, Seymour is in my English class and we've met."

"Seymour's inside painting a wall. If you girls have a

few minutes, if you really think they won't start choir practice without you, I can go get Seymour. I'm sure he'd like to say hello."

I was sure I'd like to say good-bye. Andrea was going to wreck everything. The party invitation *plus* this "chance" meeting would be too much.

"I'm afraid it would make us too late for choir practice," I said. Then I said, "Awfully nice meeting you, Mr. Finkelstein," and I turned around and walked away.

He said, "Nice meeting you, Daisy."

That sounded good to me. I didn't want him telling Seymour he had met a girl named Dana in front of his house. How many Danas are there around who, in addition, are in Seymour's English class? I was sorry I had spilled that, but I wasn't about to get caught up in any lies.

Andrea, to my surprise, ran after me. We started to walk home.

"Why did you do that?" I asked.

"I did it for you, kiddo," she said. "Just for you."

11

My party was now just a few days away. I had given up hope that anything exciting would happen with Seymour before then. But one day, out of the blue, I made it happen. It was in English class.

We were still on contemporary authors, and everybody had a chance to name their favorite contemporary author if they had one. I was anxious to see whom Seymour would name. Then maybe I could read a bunch of that author's books and have something really meaty to discuss with Seymour. That seemed more sensible than most of my Seymour ideas.

I kept waiting for our English teacher to call on Seymour. I thought it would never happen, because Clint Davis, who is very long-winded, got up to talk about Shakespeare. Ms. Tree gently reminded Clint that Shakespeare wasn't exactly contemporary, but

Clint replied, "Well, I'm contemporary and Shakespeare was an author, so you put us both together and there you are." Clint is also something of a wise guy.

Nobody was much interested in Shakespeare, because he seemed like an ancient relative who was dumped on you when you were very young before you got a chance to decide whether you liked him or not. By the time you got to his good qualities, you were sick and tired of him. Unless you were Clint Davis.

Finally Ms. Tree got around to Seymour, who didn't seem overly pleased to be gotten around to. He spoke very quietly and very respectfully to the ceiling. "I don't have a favorite contemporary author," he said.

"Fair enough," said Ms. Tree evenly, although it wasn't the kind of answer she was crazy about getting. Ms. Tree always tries to be tactful. Sometimes tact screams.

I could tell that Seymour was embarrassed by Ms. Tree's trying-to-be-ever-so-cool answer. He probably would have felt better if she had blasted him: "Now, Seymour, you be sure to get yourself a favorite contemporary author by tomorrow. Don't you dare walk into this classroom without one!"

I could rescue Seymour from his bad moment. All I had to do was raise my hand. Ms. Tree always paid attention to me. I was one of her better students. She would welcome my raised hand. And so would Seymour.

I raised my hand.

"Yes, Dana, who is *your* favorite contemporary author?"

Ms. Tree clearly anticipated an answer loaded with significance.

I went blank. Lately I had been on a binge of reading the classics. I'm not really freaked out on classics or anything like that, but I go through these stages. But now I had to think contemporary, and fast.

Ms. Tree was waiting. In my next breath, she knew, I would name an author with the right credentials— alienation from our materialistic contemporary society, coupled with an individualistic point of view, sprinkled with wit and smothered in onions. I was in trouble. My mind was collapsing under the weight of Ms. Tree's expectations.

"Buzz Janos, the author of *Tennis with Buzz!*" I announced proudly. The madness was not abating. I hadn't read nor even seen *Tennis with Buzz*. But Buzz certainly was my favorite contemporary author.

Everyone was screaming with laughter. Including Seymour Finkelstein. I felt like a folk hero.

Ms. Tree seemed not to have heard of *Tennis with Buzz*. It wasn't in her literary league. But she was willing to give me the benefit of the doubt. "That *almost* sounds like a sports book, Dana," she said cheerfully. And a little tentatively.

"It is," I said. "And it's a best seller, too."

Ms. Tree didn't think much of best sellers.

"But it doesn't have any sex in it," I added. I just assumed it wouldn't.

Someone in the back of the room applauded.

"Now, really, Dana, I think you could come up with a more appropriate author," said Ms. Tree.

"What's inappropriate about Buzz Janos?" I asked. I couldn't believe how daring I had become. But I could just imagine Buzz cheering me on.

"My favorite contemporary author is John Updike," said Laurie Bickford from the front row.

No one had asked. But Ms. Tree was elated to be going from Buzz Janos to John Updike. I was an easy act to follow, and Laurie scored big with Ms. Tree.

Seymour turned all the way around and grinned at me. I grinned back. It was the strongest connection between us so far.

I was somewhere between the class heroine and the class idiot. But I never did find out just where.

12

The bright-green shirt, the one made from silk spun by worms who hadn't thought much about consumer care, was my choice to wear at the party. I paired it with plain jeans, so that if half of me looked like I had tried too hard, the other half wouldn't.

Mom and Dad helped me pull the party together, picking out food, paper plates, and all that stuff. Andrea came over Saturday afternoon to help, too. But she had to leave early to do her hair. Jennifer came by later to pitch in. I was touched by that. Jennifer had her own date that night, and she certainly didn't *have* to help me with my party. Maybe there was a reason, in addition to living next door to her, for my thinking of Jennifer as a friend. I had a sudden urge to talk to Mom about trying to like Jennifer. Jennifer worked hard for the party. That made me feel that she was a better friend to me than I was to her. She actually apologized when she had to leave to get ready for her own date. Mom seemed sorry to see Jennifer go. I guess Mom was liking her, too. Something good was coming out of the party and it hadn't even begun. I was optimistic.

Kids started to arrive before eight. Would you believe that for a while I got so busy with them that I actually forgot the purpose of the party, the main attraction? One of the boys said he liked my shirt. The worms would have been proud. I kept alert for any news about the debating team, hoping I wouldn't hear anything about a last-minute cancellation of their out-of-town debate. By eight thirty, I felt secure that they wouldn't be coming. But I also began to worry that Seymour wouldn't show up. Thirty minutes had gone by and not a sign of him. Andrea and I exchanged anxious looks. I noticed that Andrea looked particularly nice. She was wearing a blue velour skirt and vest outfit. Andrea hates makeup, but that night she must have forgotten. She looked almost beautiful. I was glad she was on my side.

Suddenly I saw Andrea's expression change. I didn't know what it meant. But then I did. I saw Seymour coming toward me. Someone had let him in.

"Hi," he said.

"Hi," I said.

I wished he had called me by name.

"Sorry I'm late," he said. "I was fixing my car this afternoon and I lost track of time."

At last he was sharing a tiny bit of information about his life. I already knew he had spent the previous Saturday afternoon painting a wall in his house.

"That's okay," I said. "Want something to eat or drink?"

"Not now," he said. "I had a late supper."

More information.

I didn't know what to say next. But I didn't have to think about it because there was Andrea rushing toward us. When she got to my side, she just stood there, looking up at Seymour. Naturally she was waiting for me to introduce her.

"Andrea, this is Seymour Finkelstein. He moved here—um—a while ago." (I knew exactly how long ago, but I didn't want Seymour to know I had kept track.)

Well, talk about toothy smiles. From somewhere in the back of Andrea's mouth, from reserves heretofore hidden from me, emerged the whitest, gleamiest, broadest smile I'd ever seen. I swear I had never seen this smile come out of Andrea before.

"Hello," said Seymour. Now Andrea had a *hello* from Seymour.

"I think I've seen you around school," Seymour said. "Do you have second-period math with Mr. Lodge? Wait, no. It must have been somewhere else. I don't remember you in any of my classes."

In just a few moments Andrea had gotten more out of Seymour than I had in weeks of scheming. And she didn't seem to mind one bit. Could this be happening?

"I'm not in any of your classes," Andrea said. "I *know* I would have remembered you."

How could she come on to him like that! I was getting hot under my green silk shirt. I stood there reassessing my entire relationship with Andrea. I had known her since the beginning of the school year. She had moved here from Virginia. Great. She and Seymour were both relative newcomers to town, both nostalgic for people and places left forever behind. Andrea had made friends with me right away. She was fun, and I thought she had an undercurrent of loyalty. But you never really know.

"It's the debating team!" somebody screamed. I froze. Then I turned around. There they were, the whole articulate bunch of them. Well, maybe it wasn't the entire team, but it sure looked like it as they streamed into my house. I was glad Mom and Dad weren't home. Sometimes they stay upstairs during my parties, but usually they go out. They trust me.

The party became a blur. So many kids. So much noise. My stereo was blasting away. Food and drinks were all over the floor. Seymour drifted off to talk to a guy, and Andrea busied herself helping to fill up empty bowls with food. I got myself a ginger ale because my throat felt dry, and then I sat down in my father's favorite chair.

"Hey, this is a great party, Dana." It was Seymour.

"I guess so," I said. I felt drained and tired of trying.

"Don't you feel good?" he asked.

Suddenly I did. Things were getting personal at last.

"Yeah, I feel fine," I said. "So. How do you like living here? How do you like school?"

"Everything's strange. And I'm always making comparisons with my old place and my old friends."

"Have you made many new friends here?" I was liking this conversation. We were getting *into* things.

"Some. Being a new guy has its . . ."

Seymour never finished. Because Andrea waltzed over.

"Don't let me interrupt," she said.

After that everything got strained. I said something. Andrea said something. Seymour said something. Around and around we went. Why didn't Andrea leave! Why did she come over in the first place when she saw Seymour and me finally alone? I knew why. I felt sick. Andrea was after Seymour, and worse, she knew all my plans and schemes about him. In fact, she had made some of them herself. What if she told him? What if she told him that this party, which turned out to be a big party, was in fact supposed to be a small party thrown for the one and only purpose of my getting to know Seymour? What if she told him and left out *her* part of it!

I excused myself and went over to talk to members of the debating team.

At last kids started to leave the party. When Seymour left, he thanked me. Very enthusiastically, very sincerely. If I hadn't been crazy about him before, I was now. The *thank you* jelled with his broad shoulders. But I was nowhere with him. Because of Andrea. Andrea left soon after Seymour did. Usually when I have a party, she waits until everyone leaves and then we talk, talk, talk about it. She said, "I'd like to stay longer, but I promised I'd be home early because my folks are going out early tomorrow morning and they don't want to be disturbed late at night." Or she said some kind of garbled thing like that. Who cares?

At one o'clock in the morning I stood in the middle of the grungy mess of my party, which was now officially over. I vowed important things, like I would never wear the product of worms again because it's obviously bad luck.

13

Why had Andrea done what she had done? Maybe she hadn't done anything. Maybe she had just been trying to be friendly to Seymour. It was the morning after the party, and my head was foggy.

I needed to confide in someone. And this wasn't a job for Melvin. I could write a letter to Kim clear across the country, or call her and blow a whole month's allowance. But it's hard to confide long distance. You get quickie reactions and answers.

There was my sort of friend, Ingrid Silver. Once she had done me a small but crucial favor. She had gone out on a date for me with Judd Evergreen, whom I couldn't stand. I had accepted the date out of stupidity, and then totally chickened out. But I couldn't bring myself to break it. Judd Evergreen has the kind of face that never recovers from disappointment.

Every blow to his ego is etched there forever. Anyway, Ingrid had gone out on the date in my place, telling Judd that I had come down with "this rare strain of an exotic virus." Only God and Judd seemed to know what that was, and he cheerfully accepted the excuse. Would you believe it, Judd and Ingrid became a steady pair. Ingrid never let me forget what she had done for me. Actually I had done *her* a favor by getting her together with forever-etched Judd Evergreen. But Ingrid works on a credit and debit system, and I realized that if I confided in her about Andrea, she'd make me owe her even more.

I was down to Jennifer and my parents. Mom and Dad were getting anxious that their contract wouldn't be renewed, and they were still having problems with obnoxious Mr. Carlin. So this wasn't the time to dump anything on them.

Jennifer. Should I confide in her about Andrea and Seymour? Since the cafeteria fight she and Andrea had been icy toward each other. She'd be prejudiced. Also, maybe Jennifer liked Seymour. Hadn't she been kind of dreaming over him that afternoon at my house? I felt confused.

The telephone interruped my thoughts. It was Andrea. "You threw a big party after all," she said. "And your Seymour is something else."

My Seymour? Why did she put it that way?

I had to say something. "You liked him?"

"Sure. What's not to like? Are you going to see him again?"

"I haven't seen him the first time. That is, he's never asked me out."

"Do you think he will now? Did he say anything? Did he hint?"

What was Andrea's motive? Was she a friend or a rival? I wasn't sure what to think.

I didn't answer.

"You still like him, don't you?"

Andrea sounded like she *had* to know.

"I'm not sure," I lied. I just knew I never wanted to confide anything in Andrea again. I changed the subject.

On Monday I had a pleasant surprise at school. Before English class Seymour came over. He was very friendly. "Have you recovered from your party?" he asked.

I shrugged.

"Do you give many parties?" He was trying to make conversation.

"Well, now and then."

Was he going to ask me out?

"Well, this one sure was cool. The whole debating team. How did you manage to get all of them?" Seymour scratched his head. Then he went to his seat without waiting for an answer.

Things were moving backward and forward and standing still all at the same time. I had a new limbo feeling about Seymour. I was better off with *hello*, when the future still stretched ahead. Now I seemed stuck in the quicksand of polite conversation.

14

In the days following the party, Andrea sort of slunk out of sight. It wasn't the kind of physical slinking that Melvin does, but still it seemed almost furtive. I saw her at school, but when I telephoned her at home she couldn't come over, and didn't ask me over, and sometimes she wasn't even home. I wondered if she was avoiding me on purpose or if she was just suddenly busy with something or someone or what. I didn't make a big deal of it. I didn't say a word. I figured that whatever it was would either blow over or come to a head.

But it kept bothering me. Maybe I had hurt her feelings. Maybe I had said something I shouldn't have said. I decided to corner her at school. I sat down beside her in the cafeteria. "Is there something wrong? Are you mad at me?" I came right out with it.

Andrea looked at me in a kind of blank way. "No."

"I think you're avoiding me."

"Well, I'm not. This is just a hectic time for me."

"I still think you're avoiding me."

"Look, I'm going downtown today. Want to come? I'm buying some new clothes and I'd love to get your opinion."

"Sure."

If Andrea had really wanted my opinion, she would have come up to me or called me and asked me to go downtown with her. But later on that day, as we walked around town together, everything seemed to be back to normal between us. My doubts about Andrea started to fade. She seemed to be the same old Andrea. Except that she was excited about clothes. This was something new. We went from store to store. She tried on one outfit after another.

"What do you need all this stuff for?" I asked when we were in our sixth dressing room. She was trying on a red dress. She had already bought three new things.

"I just need them," she said. "Does this make me look fat?"

"No."

"Thin?"

"How do you want to look?"

"Smashing."

"You do. It's a great dress."

It was. I wanted it myself.

"Okay," she said. "This is it. I'm finished."

"Glad to hear it. Because I have to take these jeans back to Leed's." I held up the package I had been carrying around.

"Leed's? That's four blocks from here. And I'm beat."

"But we're downtown and I want to get rid of these jeans."

"You don't need *me* for that."

I was getting mad, but I didn't want to show it. I had dragged around for hours with Andrea, and now she didn't have any time for me. I shrugged. "Well, I can do it some other time."

We caught a bus home. As we rode along, Andrea with her packages high in her lap, and I holding my one package and one of Andrea's, I realized that there had been something strange about the afternoon. Something missing. Andrea hadn't asked me one question about Seymour. Not one. The whole afternoon, in fact, was out of focus. All the clothes. No questions. It should have been all the questions and no clothes. Andrea always made fun of people who bought a lot of clothes.

"Have you seen Seymour?"

The question came from me.

"Seymour?"

"It's an easy question, Andrea. It's on a par with who's buried in Grant's Tomb. No sweat."

"Are you being sarcastic?"

"No, but how come you're not asking me anything about him?"

"I did. The day after the party. But you acted like it was none of my business."

Andrea was right.

"I guess I did. But you seemed to be coming on to him at the party."

"Well, I wasn't. Seymour and I are just friends."

"*Friends?* You and Seymour are friends? How can that be when you only talked with him for a few minutes at my party and you don't have any classes with him and you don't live near him? You have no geographical or educational or social connection to Seymour."

"You sound like a lawyer."

"Is that your answer?"

"Okay. I had to call him up about something and then I had to see him just once about the something I called him up about."

"*You* don't sound like a lawyer. You sound like the CIA. What's the big secret?"

"No secret. But I don't have to tell you everything. If you don't trust me, what's our friendship all about?"

Good question.

15

I thought about Andrea. I *wanted* to trust her. I called her a couple of nights after our shopping trip. I was feeling lonely. I had to make my own supper. A cream cheese sandwich. Mom and Dad had a late taping. Even Melvin was asleep.

"Hi," I said.

"Hi."

"Doing anything special?"

"Well, homework."

"Good. Come over here and do it. My folks are out."

"I can't."

"Can't?"

"I'm just freaked out over this homework assignment. But I think I'm getting somewhere. If I go out, I'll break the spell."

"Sure."

"My parents will kill me if I flunk this course."

"Right."

I got off the phone as quickly as I could. Almost the minute I hung up, I heard my parents come in.

"Dana!"

They were forever calling to me from downstairs when I was upstairs. I went downstairs.

"Sorry we were out so long. What did you make for supper?" Dad expected a dull answer.

He got it. "A cream cheese sandwich."

"That's what I thought. Look, Mom and I had a mediocre supper, too. So let's all go out for a snack."

That sounded perfect to me. I got my coat. Mom and Dad hadn't even taken theirs off. Out we went.

We went to Luigi's Lair. It's just about the most popular eating place in town for all ages. It has a bunch of little rooms, each with a different name, each containing cozy booths dripping in plants. The whole city can be eating there and still it feels private. Sometimes it looked as if the whole city *was* eating there, it was so crowded.

We didn't have to wait too long for a table. Mom and Dad waved to someone they knew as we were going to our booth. I saw a couple of kids from school at another booth. Our booth was under what looked like a man-eating plant. I felt it. It was alive.

My parents ordered a drink to start. While they were drinking, I excused myself to go to the ladies' room. I had left the house so fast, I hadn't combed my hair or checked to see if my face was clean. The ladies' room was crowded as usual. I stood in back of two women who were standing in front of a full-length mirror. From that distance, and with them partially blocking the view, I looked fine.

Just then the door to the ladies' room swung open and in walked Andrea. She was wearing the red dress I had helped her pick out. I think I gasped. I think she did, too, when she saw me. Her hand went up to her face and then backed off. What in the world was she doing here? One of us had to say something, so I started things off.

"Finished your homework already?"

"Uh, I figured I needed a break. And I called you before I came here, but there wasn't any answer."

"Oh. You here with your folks?"

"Uh, yuh." Andrea was having trouble opening her mouth.

"Where?"

"You mean in what room?"

"Yeah, what room? I'm here with my folks, too. Maybe we could all eat together in one booth."

"I don't know what room we're in. What room are you in?"

"The Florentine Macho Room." (All of Luigi's rooms have strange names that sound as if someone drunk made them up.)

"I don't know where that room is," said Andrea, as if that settled everything. She turned to go. "Well, I'll be missed if I don't get back. See you tomorrow, Dana."

I was mad. I felt that I had let Andrea get away with something. But I had to think about it, all the angles. I had left my house right after I had talked with Andrea. Andrea lives about the same distance from the restaurant as I do. About five minutes by car. I'd been at the restaurant about ten minutes, including waiting time. Andrea probably arrived at the waiting area right after my folks and I were shown to our booths. Otherwise we would have seen her. My guess was that Andrea had left her house soon after talking to me. And here she was wearing that new red dress. Is that what she does her homework in? It didn't add up. Also, she swung in and out of the ladies' room in the fastest round trip I've ever seen. Whatever she had come into the ladies' room to do, she had changed her mind when she had seen me.

I decided to take the long way back to my booth. I walked slowly through the Mona Lisa's Grandpa Room, the Mediterranean Misfit Room, and the main room, which was Luigi's Lust. I looked hard for Andrea. Was she really with her parents? Was she with *Seymour*? Was that why she was avoiding me? It couldn't be. Could it? I didn't find her. I wondered if she had left immediately after seeing me.

I went back to my parents' booth. They were discussing the menu. They really looked like a class act. Sometimes when we go to a restaurant they're recognized, and we get fawned over and we get the best table if it's empty. Some of the restaurant owners think my parents are connected to the restaurant critic at the station. I sat down. I didn't say anything about seeing Andrea.

I studied the menu. Some of the names of the dishes were nuttier than the names of the rooms, but the food was usually very good. We all ordered the same thing. I no longer remember what.

But it was fun being out with my parents. We talked quite a bit about Buzz Janos, and how they were looking forward to his visit. I tried not to show how much I was looking forward to it. But in trying not to, I did.

The food came pretty fast. But right in the middle of my meal, I asked to be excused again. I *had* to make another tour of the place. I *had* to see who Andrea was with. I thought about asking the kids from school whom I had seen in a booth. They were still there. But that would make me seem like a snoop.

I still couldn't find Andrea. This increased my suspicion that she had left immediately after seeing me. This also increased my suspicion that she had something—or someone—to hide from me. I went back to my booth.

"Are you a bit jumpy tonight, Dana?" Dad asked.

"Yeah, I guess so," I said.

"Something on your mind?"

"Yeah, but it's not worth talking about."

"Well, if it ever gets worth talking about, we'll be glad to listen," Mom said.

Dad nodded.

"I know," I said.

I finished my meal. My parents were already

through with theirs. We ordered dessert and coffee. "This was some snack," I said.

"I think we were all starved," Mom said.

When we got home I went to my room and dialed Andrea's number. I had made up my mind in the restaurant that I would do it. I was getting paranoid thinking that Andrea might be with Seymour. I was probably overreacting. A phone call would make things right.

"Hello."

Andrea's mother answered.

"Oh, hi, Mrs. Motts. Gee, I'm sorry I missed seeing you at Luigi's tonight."

"You missed seeing me? What do you mean? I wasn't there." Mrs. Motts was borderline frantic.

"You weren't? Uh, is Andrea home?"

"No, she's out for the evening. Any message? I can give her a message. No trouble."

"No, that's okay. I'll see her tomorrow."

It wouldn't have mattered whether I gave Mrs. Motts a message or not. She was terrible at delivering messages. But she always liked to get them. Information was what she was after. I knew there was only a small chance she would tell Andrea that I had called. Andrea would think she had gotten away with whatever she had gotten away with. I still didn't know what it was. And I wasn't going to say anything to Andrea until I found out.

But I knew that something had left our friendship that would never come back.

16

I'm good at scenarios. My imagination is so active that I can put scenes together with all the actors and props and tell how things are going to come out. Of course I was able to come up with a comparison of what it would be like for Seymour to be dating Andrea and for Seymour to be dating me. I came out far ahead.

First, I could see Seymour calling for Andrea. Her parents, Mr. and Mrs. Motts, are home because Mr. and Mrs. Motts are steadfast homebodies, especially when they want to size up Andrea's latest. Mr. and Mrs. Motts are respectable people, but Mrs. Motts is a little nuts and Mr. Motts has a thing about roaches. Not a little quirk, but an honest-to-goodness *thing*. I would, too, if I lived in their house. It's crawling. Mr. and Mrs. Motts are socially mortified about this, because middle-class homes are not supposed to be havens for the crawlies. But I understand that once roaches set up housekeeping in your place, it's hard to get them out. The Mottses have gone into the roach real estate business.

Enter Seymour. Unsuspecting Seymour. He gets a perfectly normal *hello* from Mr. and Mrs. Motts, although he wonders vaguely why they both have to meet him at the door. He doesn't know about Andrea's adventures with Planned Parenthood. Or was it Family Planning? Well, it doesn't matter. Andrea likes to call some of these "planned" organizations. They don't want to know your last name, only your first, and Andrea thinks that's all very conspiratorial and funny. Mrs. Motts overheard one of the calls, and she became nearly hysterical with fear. Now she and Mr. Motts watch everyone who calls for Andrea at the house.

But they're pleasant enough to Seymour, because although he's handsome, he has an innocent air about him. They invite him to sit down and wait for Andrea. Seymour sits down and a roach climbs up his leg.

Mr. Motts goes after it. "You crazy nut! You dirty rat!" he yells. "I'll get you, you blankety blankety blank!" Mr. Motts routinely swears at roaches.

Then Mrs. Motts starts asking Seymour questions. Personal questions. (After all, she belongs to the legions of the chronically frantic.) "Are you familiar with Planned Parenthood, and if so, why?" Well, maybe not that personal, but *personal*, believe me.

Seymour is now squirming, partially from the roach, partially from the questions.

Andrea comes into the room. She looks nice. All right, I'll have to admit it, she looks smashing. Lately Andrea has turned into a butterfly. But Seymour is wondering whether it's all worth it. The End. We leave Seymour with serious doubts about Andrea Motts.

Now, Seymour is calling for *me*. Only one person answers the door. Whoever is handy, nothing pre-planned. Melvin is right at the door, too, with a friendly wag of his tail. Let's say that Mom is the one who answers the door. She invites Seymour into our roach-free living room and they chat pleasantly. Easy topics like school, politics, the weather. Seymour feels right at home and, for an added bonus, is happy to be talking *in person* to a TV star. Maybe it's unfair to compare Mom's conversation with Mrs. Motts's. After all, Mom is a professional talker.

Seymour feels something on his leg. But it is only Melvin, snuggling up to him. Everything is warm and cozy and comfortable.

I come into the room. I smile at Seymour. No butter-fly, let's face it. But I look very appealing to Seymour. The End. We leave Seymour happy that he has made the right choice. Me, Dana Small.

I felt smug about the scenes I had created in my head. Life should be a series of self-created scenes. Especially when they're on target, like mine. Of course

Andrea might come up with a somewhat different version. Seymour would sweep her up in his arms, rescuing her from the roach-infested floor of her living room, and carry her away to an officially sanitized home, with those strips of paper used in motel bathrooms. Only in this home everything has a sanitized paper strip—lamps, stoves, beds, curtains, the works. "You deserve this," Seymour says to Andrea. "You deserve sanitized love."

Then both of them call Planned Parenthood because they're so in love they're really going to need some advice.

That possibility drives me up the wall.

So long, scenario.

17

During the next week I had to push Andrea to the back of my mind. Things were heating up in my parents' situation. For them, everything was getting clearer. Their problem, their one and only real problem, was Mr. Carlin. It was becoming obvious that he wanted them *out*. "He probably has a nephew somewhere who's just itching to become a TV host," my father joked.

I was worried. This was our future. We weren't rich, and jobs in TV didn't come along every minute. My parents didn't even have college educations, so it would be hard for them to work outside their field. They had met in drama school, been in Broadway plays together, and had bit parts in movies and a few starring roles on TV. But this show was everything to them. There was always talk of syndicating it, but nothing ever came of it. So they were stuck with its being simply local, and they were stuck with Mr. Carlin. And now their old contract was running out.

On Friday my parents practically stormed into the house. "We were just introduced to Carlin's new lawyer," Dad said. "He sits there, looks me straight in the eye, and recites with absolute conviction a bunch of drivel that he knows isn't true."

Mom spoke up. "In short, Dana, we've been offered a rotten contract. I think I've figured out Carlin's strategy. He couldn't refuse to offer us a new contract. Our ratings are too high. How could he explain it to his stockholders or financial backers or whoever helped him buy the station? But he can offer us a bad deal that seems like a good deal, and when we refuse it he'll just say he couldn't come to terms with stubborn us. Our lawyer and his lawyer will be back and forth and back and forth on it, but when the smoke clears Dad and I will be out."

"But he doesn't have a replacement."

"Yes, he does," said my father. "His nephew."

"But that's a joke. You're always kidding about that. You don't mean there really *is* a nephew?"

"There really is a nephew," said Mom.

Suddenly we all started to laugh. It was hilarious. It was sad.

"So what are you going to do about the contract?" I asked.

"We simply don't know," said Mom.

I changed the subject.

I had been staying away from the studio as much as possible. In fact, I hadn't been there since I had seen *my* TV show. I did finally go to the station with Mom and Dad because we were going out to dinner right after their taping with a local botany professor. But the professor didn't show. He called to say he was stuck in traffic and would be late. There was nothing for me to do but read TV magazines and feed coins into the junk food machines. At last Mom said, "We have to wait for this guy, but you don't. You're not hungry anymore, are you? Why don't you go home. Maybe Mr. Carlin will drive you. It's on his way."

"I'll wait," I said.

"You've got homework to do," Dad said. "And it's dark, so we'd rather you didn't go alone."

I groaned.

The timing was perfect. Or imperfect, depending on your point of view. Mr. Carlin was just about to leave. I said good-bye to my parents, and Mr. Carlin and I walked silently to his car. He opened the front door for me, which astonished me. Maybe rude people have their own kind of manners. They'll yell and scream at you, but they won't grab the last piece of cake if they know you want it.

We started off and I asked him if he knew where I lived and he said he did. Then he asked, "How have you been?"

He was in a wonderful mood!

"Fine, thank you. How have you been?"

"Just fine."

"Why?"

"Why what?"

"Why have you been just fine?"

Mr. Carlin half looked at me and half kept his eyes on the road. "Are you putting me on? What kind of question is that?"

"I was just wondering if you feel fine because you think you're kicking my folks out of the station."

"Listen, kid—"

"I'm not a kid."

"Yes, you are. Otherwise you wouldn't have made that juvenile crack when you were on TV. Where do you get off being such an expert? An expert wise guy."

Mr. Carlin was getting furious.

I didn't answer. Maybe I was a wise guy. Or maybe just dumb for getting into an argument with someone driving a lethal instrument, which is my definition of a car. But Mr. Carlin didn't say anything else. He just drove along grimly. The combination of his hostility and the car and the darkness frightened me. Suddenly he stopped the car.

"Why are you stopping?" I asked. I must have heard that line a million times on TV and in the movies just before this really cretin girl who stupidly got into a car in the first place with a homicidal maniac gets attacked. Usually there's a blackout before the question is answered. Next thing you know there's a sheet-covered body being wheeled into an ambulance, and police-car lights are flashing all over the place, and middle-aged and elderly people in nightclothes are standing around and gawking. At this point a really handsome but somewhat hard-bitten guy, probably an investigative reporter or a detective, takes over. Sometimes, I've noticed, the guy looks like a slightly older version of Seymour Finkelstein. This Seymour Finkelstein type avenges the girl, whom he falls in love with even though she's dead, by seeing that her killer spends the declining years of his life making license plates and potholders while the sun flickers in through the bars of his cell. Seymour Finkelstein. Hero. Avenger. Dispenser of justice.

"This *is* your house, isn't it?" Mr. Carlin was talking.

We were in front of my house! Mr. Carlin had delivered me safely. He leaned over and opened the door for me. "Stay away from the station, will you, kid? That's an order. Juveniles and minors give me the creeps."

"*Creeps* give me the creeps, Mr. Carlin!" I said. I hoped he got it. He drove off.

I was grinning. I was elated by my stupidity. I had effectively gotten myself banished from the TV station forever.

18

Seymour and I were talking almost every day at school. Every day I hoped he would ask me out, but he didn't. Every day turned into a disappointment. I wanted to stop hoping, but I couldn't.

At home things were picking up. Mom and Dad were making plans for Buzz's return to town. His schedule kept getting changed, and his visit kept getting postponed. But in the works were at least two, maybe three, TV shows totally devoted to him, with my parents alternating as hosts. There was also an autographing at Leed's, and press conferences. I was getting anxious to see Buzz again. I wondered what would happen when I did. When you haven't seen someone for a while, you either take up just where you left off or you have to start all over again.

When Buzz finally came to town, he showed up at

our house with the same two guys. Mom told me to answer the door. I think she'd planned it that way.

Buzz gave me a toothy *hi* and took my hand. He said, "How've you been?"

I forgot to say hello to the two guys with him.

I can't remember what I said to Buzz. I just remember all of us sitting around the living room again as if we'd never left it. This time, though, I hung around while plans for Buzz's personal appearances were discussed. Most of the talk concerned the tapings he'd be making with Mom and Dad.

Mom had read in a sports magazine that Buzz was crazy about homemade carrot cake. Mom's cake was from the freezer at the supermarket, but nothing's perfect.

After the business talk was over—and it went on forever—everyone loosened up and stretched out. We all seemed to be talking at once. The agent and the agent's agent (they were really promotion and publicity people) were fun. I hadn't paid any attention to them the first time they were at my house. While I was talking I kept staring at Buzz's profile. I was a little surprised when the profile turned toward me and asked, "Want to go out for something?"

It seemed obvious that Buzz wanted to spend some time with me exclusively. I was elated but nervous.

Absolutely everyone smiled, including me. Then I said yes. Mom and Dad didn't come right out and say I could go out with Buzz. They vaguely nodded. That was a well-executed maneuver. After all, to come out and give me *permission* to go out with Buzz would have been the pits.

Buzz and I both stood up at the same time. "We'll be back before dawn," he said with a grin. At this point my parents looked slightly uneasy. We walked out into the night. I felt . . . flattered. That was what I felt. And why not? This celebrity liked me. I almost laughed to myself when I thought how hard I had tried to get Seymour Finkelstein, a certifiable non-celebrity, to ask me out. What a strange world.

"There's a pizza place a few blocks from here," I said after we got into the car Buzz was using. "They serve coffee. The coffee's better than the pizza."

"Maybe I'll be courageous and try both," he said, and he laughed.

I directed Buzz to the pizza place. Maybe it was a mistake. Music was blasting, and it was all so *teen-aged*. But Buzz seemed to like it. We ordered plain pizzas and coffee. I really wanted a Coke, but I didn't want to seem young. Then we sat down in a booth and waited. Buzz was staring at me.

"I'm going to come right out and say this," he said. "And I hope you won't think it's a line. But there's a quality about you that's tremendously appealing. . . ."

"Oh?"

"I know that I don't *really* know you, but . . ." Buzz's voice trailed off.

I believed Buzz. I knew he was attracted to me. I

was too young for him, but I didn't care. I also knew that I might never hear from him after he left town. I was a girl in a city that he was visiting and then leaving forever. His social life was all about meeting and leaving girls. But that didn't matter right now. We were friends and it felt natural. It felt much better than trying too hard for Seymour Finkelstein. I, Dana Small, was above that sort of thing.

I felt mature about coming to that realization. I felt grateful to Buzz for helping me come to it even though he didn't have the faintest idea that he had helped me become a sensible human being. I felt wise and relaxed and thoroughly happy, even looking forward to what I knew was going to be a vile pizza.

And then Andrea walked in on the arm of Seymour Finkelstein.

19

Andrea was as shocked to see me with a celebrity as she was shocked that I had caught her with Seymour. Seymour was wide-eyed over everything. He stared at Buzz and me. I loved it, I loved it. But I hated seeing him with Andrea. Was this their first date? I didn't think so. I remembered Luigi's Lair. How long had this been going on?

"Could I have your autograph?" It was Seymour, asking Buzz—*my* date—for an autograph. Watching Buzz sign his name on a napkin that said *PIZZA, PLEAZ,* was heaven for me. Andrea looked down. She was avoiding my eyes.

I smiled. "Buzz and I are just goofing off before his round of personal appearances this weekend."

Buzz seemed to realize he was in the middle of a sticky situation. "Yes," he said. "I don't know what I'd do without Dana. She's making being here so interesting and so much fun."

Buzz took my hand. We were now partners. Oh, joy!

Seymour was staring at me. But it was like he was looking at me for the very first time. You've heard the expression looking at someone with new eyes. Well, Seymour's eyes were so brand-new they looked newly minted.

I got the feeling that Andrea was fading away. Now she was an outsider to what seemed to me a delicious little triangle.

At last Seymour and Andrea walked on to a booth. Everything that I had ever felt for Seymour was suddenly transferred to Buzz. I was in trouble again. But maybe, after Buzz left town, it would pass. Maybe I could be sane again and not have a thing for him *or* Seymour.

Buzz and I sat there silently. It was awkward. I said, "I guess you're wondering what that was all about. Did you ever have a friend who really wasn't a friend?"

"Are you kidding? What do you think happens to me when I travel around? I meet people who are anxious to be my friend—put friend in quotes—just because I'm . . . because of my tennis name. They want to use me in some way. For every hundred people I meet, maybe ten are sincere."

"Did you figure that out mathematically?"

"I sit around hotel rooms a lot and it gets monotonous, so I play all kinds of statistical games. It beats doing crossword puzzles."

"So, statistically you land up with ten friends out of one hundred?"

"No. Sometimes none out of one hundred. Other factors go into it. The vibes have to be right, then throw in chemistry, empathy . . ."

"You make it sound tremendously hard to find even one real friend."

"Isn't it?"

Just then the pizzas came and Buzz and I began to eat. He didn't ask me anything about Andrea and Seymour, and that made me like him all the more. I wondered if he guessed that Seymour was important to me. Or *had* been important to me.

We stayed in the pizza place two hours. Andrea and Seymour left before us, Seymour glancing and nodding as they passed our booth. Andrea looked straight ahead.

When Buzz and I got into his car to drive home, I felt depressed. I knew I'd be seeing him off and on during the weekend, but then it would be over. Over as if it hadn't even happened. When we reached my house, we got out of the car. The house was dark.

"I guess your friends went back to your hotel without you," I said. "Mom and Dad probably gave them a ride."

"I forgot about them," he said.

"It must have been the fabulous pizza," I said.

"No, more likely your company, Dana."

We walked up to the door. I tried it to make sure it was unlocked. It was.

Buzz and I stood facing each other. I didn't think I should invite him inside. I guess he didn't think so either. He said, "I'll see you tomorrow."

Then he bent down to kiss me. I felt that Buzz and Seymour were both kissing me. That I was, in fact, being kissed by everyone I had ever hoped to be kissed by in the universe. It felt inclusive and exclusive at the same time.

20

The weekend was beautiful. Seymour and Andrea stabilized in my mind as legitimate zeroes. And Buzz and I had a fantastic time.

First there was his autographing at Leed's Department Store. I had never been to an autographing, never asked *anybody* for an autograph, even by mail. Mom and Dad and I went with Buzz to the event. In case I'm sounding like a groupie or something, Buzz really *wanted* me there, and my parents *had* to be there. One of the tapings they were doing with Buzz was taking place right after the autographing. They were also doing one with him at an outside tennis court, even though the weather was chilly. They were doing another with him and a trio of stuffy civic leaders. That one was being done in the studio.

People started lining up at the store about an hour

before the autographing was scheduled to begin. The head of the book department hid Buzz and my parents in her office so Buzz wouldn't be overwhelmed in advance. They invited me in, but I decided to stay outside and be a plain person. I wanted to watch the mob congregate, and I wanted to look around the book department. There was a huge glossy photo of Buzz holding a tennis racket. There were piles and piles of his books on the autographing table. I picked up a copy of the book and leafed through it. Somehow, with all the excitement around Buzz, I hadn't actually gotten to see *Tennis with Buzz*.

There was a gorgeous picture of Buzz on the cover. Some of the reviews of his book were blown up to be posters. I read one. It was from a fan magazine, one of those magazines that make *you* feel like a boring little person when you read it, and like you should be grateful for this glimpse into the lives of people who really count. Here's how it went:

> The photograph on the book jacket asks the musical question, Where was this guy when warts were given out? His share went to you and me, folks. Relentlessly unblemished, excruciatingly handsome, Buzz Janos *looks* like a champ. You *want* this man to marry your daughter. However, once inside *Tennis with Buzz* you forget the face on the outside and concentrate on one of the most solid books on tennis published in the past few

years. Precise, lucid prose combined with clear photographs and diagrams make this book must reading—and keeping—for everyone from the beginning player to the seasoned pro. Neither pontifical nor condescending nor breathlessly breezy, it makes its points with old-fashioned respect. Even if he doesn't marry your daughter, spend some reading time with Buzz Janos.

Tennis with Buzz. I liked it. I learned from it. You will, too.

The review made me mad. Who needs a review that compliments you by giving insults, and insults you by giving compliments? Does that sell books?

The crowd waiting for Buzz was getting bigger. About one fourth of the people were dressed in tennis clothes. Do people ordinarily dress this way in cold weather?

Someone decided to start the autographing early. Buzz strode out to his table. Everyone sort of hushed and looked at him respectfully. People stood between two velvet-covered parallel ropes that stretched all the way into the toy department. They were in a straggly-neat line like you see in the supermarket, but they were good-natured, not grumbly, and they didn't seem to mind waiting.

Some of the people gazed at Buzz reverently, like he was a spiritual experience, as they watched him sign. "Please sign this 'To Shari from Buzz.'"

"Say, 'Greetings to another great tennis player from Buzz Janos.' "

"Write whatever you think is appropriate for an eleven-year-old girl who expects to play Wimbledon and won her last match 6–0, 6–0 and she was nine years old before she first picked up a racket."

Buzz looked bewildered by that one. A long-haired teenaged girl asked Buzz to kiss her as she shoved a copy of his book in his face. Buzz gave her a quick peck on the cheek. I hoped that wouldn't start a trend.

Suddenly I had an idea. *I* wanted an autographed book from Buzz. Badly. And I wouldn't tell him or even hint about what I'd like him to write. I bought a book from one of the salespeople, who seemed spaced out or in a fog. "This isn't normal. This isn't normal at all," she informed me. Then I went to the end of the line. I took my place in back of a bunch of ladies from a tennis club. There were about ten of them, and I could tell from their conversation that they had all come together. I hoped they wouldn't give Buzz detailed accounts about all the games they had won. They were jabbering about Buzz. They said he was "so cute." It took about half an hour for me to reach him. He almost didn't look up.

"Would you autograph this for me, please?" I asked.

He looked up. He grinned. Then he wrote something with a quick, bold scrawl. I was a little disappointed that he hadn't paused to think some deep thoughts before writing. I'd die if I got a variation of "Best Wishes." Buzz closed the book and handed it back with a wink. I felt like an insider. I felt like telling the line of people, "I'm part of this. Buzz and I are . . ." What *were* we? I was having too good a time to think about that now.

I was afraid to open the book to see what Buzz had written, just in case it wasn't special enough.

The autographing ran an hour late, and then Mom and Dad taped an interview with Buzz. The taping crew had come early to get some footage at the store. They filmed the line while I was standing in it, and I hoped I didn't look dumb.

In my opinion the autographing was the public highlight of Buzz's visit. But as much as I liked it, I was hoping we'd have some time alone. Or at least alone in public. It was hard to do. We actually went back to the pizza parlor once. But Buzz was recognized, and he ended up autographing more napkins.

My parents became a little concerned that I was spending time with someone too old for me, but they trusted Buzz. In fact, I had a hunch that *they* were confiding in him.

"Your folks are tops in what they do," Buzz said to me Sunday between appointments. "They should go into syndication. Maybe I can help. I've got some contacts."

"Syndication would be just terrific."

"I'll give it a shot," he said.

"Thank you, thank you," I said. And of course I kissed him.

I was now thinking of Buzz as somewhere between

my future husband, a kindly uncle, and the best friend I'd ever had. Confusing. I kept hoping we'd really *talk*, but there was never a chance.

And then the weekend was over. Good-bye, magic. I didn't even get to say good-bye to Buzz alone. He was outside on a downtown street with the publicists and Mom and Dad and some city officials *and* a crowd of people who had gathered the minute Buzz stepped outside. So all I got was a peck on the cheek, a handshake, and a promise that he'd keep in touch. I told him that I hadn't looked at his autograph yet. But this remark got lost in all the good-byes going around.

Then he was off to the airport. Gone.

Within seconds Andrea and Seymour snapped right back into focus. As if they were just waiting to invade my mind after Buzz left. I was back in the grimy world, with my real life still up in the air.

21

Can you mourn the loss of something you never had but only thought you had? I was mourning anyway. The end of my friendship with Andrea. Maybe it wasn't the total and complete end of it, but it was the end of what I *trusted* about it. Andrea cheated on our friendship. It wasn't my fault. I didn't ask for it. I didn't deserve it. Maybe I was just an early victim in what would become a life-long collection of Victims of Andrea Motts. I could see Andrea as a big-shot business executive specializing in her favorite disposable item—people. Next I could see her manipulating her income-tax form, creating fantasies of phony deductions and expenses so she wouldn't have to pay any taxes. She would seduce the IRS man who came to audit her records. He would be so fascinated by her that they would conspire to take tax deductions for the care and upkeep of her family's roaches. Years later I saw Andrea, full of geriatric charm, in a nursing home where she would put on her red dress, pretend she was terminal, and get the room with the best view by evicting somebody gasping his last breath. I could see Andrea doing whatever she wanted on the sly and getting away with it.

It didn't make me feel any better to think that I might be just another victim. Just one of the crowd. I was hurt, I was insulted, and worst of all, Seymour actually preferred this person, Andrea, to me. *That* was hard to take. I didn't know what to do about Andrea.

As for Seymour, I avoided him. Actually, how can you avoid somebody who isn't paying any attention to you in the first place? Our daily nothing conversations had stopped anyway. And yet, even though he really wasn't paying attention to me, I thought I noticed him looking at me when he thought I wasn't looking at him. Like before English class, and during English class, and after English class. In the old days, before I got wise, I would have thought he was interested in me, maybe trying to summon up courage to ask me out. Now I knew better.

One day Jennifer came over just to talk. I was glad to see her. Even Mom was glad to see her. But Mom quickly disappeared so Jennifer and I could be private. Jennifer started to talk about herself.

"This guy, Sam Domsky, the one who took me to the

concert, asked me out again," she said. Jennifer was so excited. "I think Sam is a beautiful name, don't you? It beats Derek by a mile."

Then I said it. Point blank. "Why should *you* be excited? You can get anyone you want."

Jennifer looked at me. "I *can*?" she asked. It was almost funny, as if this was a new idea.

She went on. "I wanted Sam to ask me out and he didn't and he didn't and he didn't and I almost gave up hoping. But then he asked me to the concert, and Dana, I think things are looking good."

I was so surprised. Jennifer had been going through the same thing with Sam that I had been going through with Seymour. Although she seemed to have made more progress.

"I've been having the same kind of problem," I said. Then it all came out. I told Jennifer everything. *Everything*. Maybe it wasn't right to tell her about Andrea. But I told her anyway.

"I wouldn't try to steal anybody from anybody," said Jennifer. "There are enough guys out there. Why latch onto a friend's? Why don't you confront Andrea? I mean, really have it out. Listen to her side of it."

"If she has a side," I said.

"Maybe you'll feel better if you get it all out," said Jennifer.

It's terrible when someone as beautiful as Jennifer also makes great sense. It isn't right to have everything. I was feeling guilty, but I really meant it when I said, "I wish you luck with Sam, but you won't need it."

Jennifer impulsively kissed me. Suddenly I loved her. Jennifer the Beautiful was as nice and comfortable to have around as Melvin.

After Jennifer left I sat and wondered if I should call Andrea. Ever since that night at the pizza place, we had avoided each other at school. Hardly like old times. But it was up to her to call *me*. After all, she was the one who had gone after the guy I liked. But I knew Jennifer was right. Andrea and I *had* to talk. I kept thinking of why I should call Andrea, and then I kept thinking of anything but.

The problem was resolved one afternoon when I was shopping. I still had the jeans to return, and I needed a new pair. After I got through with returning, I took a stack of jeans to the dressing room. I make easy work of shopping. If something feels like it fits, and it looks good from the front, that's it. I never look at myself in the mirror sideways or backward or three ways or any of the combination of ways you can look in those store mirrors. Why make gross discoveries? Those mirrors always tell you something you'd rather not know.

I had just bought my pair of jeans when I saw Andrea in a corner of the jeans department, looking into a three-way mirror. My heart started to beat faster. I knew I had to speak to her now and get it over with. I went up to her. She looked satisfied with what she had just seen from all angles. But when she saw me, her face turned sour.

"Hello, Andrea," I said.

"Hello."

Very dull, unemotional *hello*s.

"I think we should talk about things," I said.

Andrea didn't answer.

Suddenly I had to go after her. "You wanted Seymour, didn't you? You liked him from the start. From the moment you saw him. If not before, from my description."

"Hey, wait a minute," said Andrea.

"*Wait* a minute! You knew I liked him. And I saw him first."

"You don't *own* liking somebody," said Andrea. "Liking a guy isn't exclusive, like you have to take out a special permit."

"You tried to steal Seymour away from me," I said.

"I can't steal something that doesn't belong to somebody in the first place."

I was beginning to think that maybe this "talk" wasn't such a good idea. It was getting nasty. Shoppers in the department who were supposed to be looking at jeans were looking at us.

I said, "Well, you had to decide between him and me . . . which relationship meant more to you."

Andrea didn't answer. I had hit the nut of the situation. There it was. We both knew it. I went on. "You decided that he meant more to you than I did."

"But in a different way," said Andrea. "You mean more to me in a lasting kind of way. Seymour means more to me in an exciting sort of way. Next year you'll probably be my friend, and Seymour and I will have forgotten all about each other."

Andrea was not sounding very sure of Seymour. I was getting suspicious.

"You've been dating Seymour a lot?" I asked.

"Yes."

"Are you *still* dating Seymour?"

I suddenly remembered how Seymour had looked at *me* when Buzz took my hand.

"Well, I expect him to call . . ."

"*Expect?* He's dumped you?"

"Really, Dana!"

Andrea was getting angry. She was steaming. She said, "Seymour Finkelstein is a Neanderthal man! That's what he is! He has no noticeable brain development."

"But he's not your ordinary Neanderthal man," I said. "Don't forget the broad shoulders and the terrific face."

"Shut up, Dana!" Andrea snapped. "That creep hasn't called me since he saw you with that Buzz. He's trying to get up enough nerve to call you. He's called already, hasn't he?"

"Seymour hasn't called," I said quietly. I wondered if Andrea knew what she was talking about, she was so teed off.

"He'll call," said Andrea. "He thinks that Buzz Janos is some kind of god, and that it's rubbed off on you. We had a very boring conversation after we ran into you and Buzz."

"Oh? How boring?" I was sure I wouldn't have found the conversation boring at all.

But Andrea didn't answer my question. She looked at me with a sort of glum anger. What was going on in her head? No matter what she said, I knew she wasn't through with Seymour. I knew what a determined person she was. Andrea wasn't going to give up on Seymour that easily.

"I have to go," she said, and walked away.

Was she walking out of my life? I no longer cared. I needed friends, but not her kind. How odd it was that Seymour Finkelstein, with whom I had no relationship whatsoever, was the reason for this big breakup in my life. Seymour Finkelstein was *not* your ordinary Neanderthal man. Without even trying, he could make waves.

22

I call what happened next The Stalking of Seymour Finkelstein. I'd been stalking Seymour for weeks, even when I told myself I wasn't. But this stalking was being done by *Andrea*. I might add she was aided by Ingrid Silver, who was probably just in it for kicks. I knew that Andrea hadn't given up on Seymour. But I didn't know what she would do about it.

I saw Andrea and Ingrid huddle together a lot and giggle. Ingrid had taken my place as Andrea's friend. It stung. What can you count on, really, when you see a switcheroo like that? They were hatching something. Something that was connected to Seymour Finkelstein, I was sure of it. And then, just by watching, I found out what it was.

Seymour sits down at a table in the cafeteria. Ingrid comes by and sits down beside him or across from him. Ingrid can sit near any guy without his getting ideas, because it's known that she's just about married to Judd. Andrea then innocently joins Ingrid. Ingrid then leaves for reasons I can't overhear. Andrea and Seymour are left together. That's about the way it works, and there are a number of variations. I've seen Ingrid at work in the hallways, before school, after school, and she probably has dozens of locations and times I'm not aware of.

Usually after Ingrid leaves I see Andrea and Seymour laughing together. Andrea seems to be making headway. Maybe Seymour will ask her out again and they'll get back together.

Maybe not. After several days of this, it dawns on me that Andrea's plan isn't working. Seymour never comes up to her. It's always the other way around. Then after a few more days it gets even more interesting. Seymour starts to avoid Andrea. This is what happens. Ingrid shows up. Seymour leaves. Simplicity itself. He doesn't stick around for the inevitable Andrea. I don't know what excuses Seymour uses for leaving. Clearly he wants to get away.

I could see it happening, but I couldn't hear any of it. Then I saw Andrea get bolder. She dumped Ingrid as the in-between person. Andrea simply showed up wherever Seymour was. And Seymour simply walked away.

The whole thing quickly went from interesting to pathetic. I began to feel sorry for Andrea. I began to think that maybe Seymour was a worm. But maybe he, like me, had finally discovered the truth about Andrea.

I kept detached until the day Seymour walked up to me after school. Andrea was heading toward Seymour. Seymour was heading toward me. Andrea stopped when she realized that *I* was Seymour's destination. It was the ultimate stop. It was as if every plan and scheme and thought and hope she had ever had about Seymour had stopped, too.

It was almost too much for me. I felt the transference of power. From Andrea to me. It reminded me of a presidential inauguration day. She, Andrea, the current President, was passing everything wonderful to me, her successor, without wanting to. I was ascending, she was descending.

I was daydreaming again. Seymour was probably coming over to ask me what time it was. Or maybe he wanted a weather report. Perhaps he wanted to borrow my comb.

"Hey, Dana, got a minute?"

For you an eternity, but I only nodded.

"Could you do me a favor?"

A favor. I knew it. My comb was filthy and covered with knotted hair.

"Maybe I shouldn't ask."

Ask, already. I realized I was making Seymour talk to himself. I said, "I'll do you a favor if I can."

Seymour tore a piece of paper from his notebook.

"It's not for me. It's for my little brother. He wants a Buzz Janos autograph. And he'd like it to say, 'To Rip Finkelstein from his pal Buzz Janos.' Rip's his nickname. I figured you're in contact with Buzz Janos, right?"

Wrong. I had been waiting to hear from Buzz. I knew he was very busy, but still . . .

"I'll be hearing from him soon."

I'd better hear from him soon. What if I never heard from him again?

"Then could you send him this paper?" Seymour wrote down, TO RIP FINKELSTEIN FROM HIS PAL BUZZ JANOS. "Or maybe you could just ask him to write this down."

Seymour was a sweet big brother. It was a new side of him. New to me, anyway. I wanted to get the autograph for him. I took the piece of paper. "I'll try to get the autograph for your little brother," I said. "But I can't promise. Buzz is *so* busy."

I felt like a spokesman for Buzz. I wished I were.

"You and he are pretty friendly?"

Was this happening? Seymour was interested in my life. Or my life as it might brush up against, be connected to, or scrounge off, the life of Buzz Janos.

But abruptly Seymour turned his head and said, "My bus is outside. I have to run. I'll be talking to you soon, okay? Maybe on the phone."

Seymour was off to catch his bus. He never found out that my comb was filthy, and I never found out

[114]

what he would have said next if his bus hadn't come. Was he about to ask me out? I made an immediate promise that I would not try to analyze our conversation. That I would simply wait for further developments, if there were any. But if Seymour now liked me, it had something to do with my knowing Buzz. Maybe I couldn't blame Seymour for that. Was it any worse than my being turned on by Seymour's broad shoulders? Is fifteen too young to go searching for depth in yourself? Probably. What if depth turns out to be dull? Plenty of time to find that out when you're older.

Andrea watched Seymour all the time he was talking to me. Ingrid joined her. They stood side by side looking depressed. They didn't seem to have anything to say to each other. What next for Andrea? Maybe she would use her stalking powers to go after Judd Evergreen. The thought was ridiculous. Judd Evergreen was ridiculous. But Judd belonged to Ingrid, which could be temptation enough for Andrea. I didn't care.

23

WE HAVE A NIBBLE!

When I got home from school I found this message on a piece of paper propped up on the kitchen table.

Mom and Dad came home a few minutes later and didn't wait for me to ask about their nibble. They told me.

Mom said, "The CBS affiliate in town is very, and I mean *very*, interested in taking on our show. We just came from an interview with them."

Dad said, "For a change *we're* being interviewed."

"Looking for another situation isn't nearly as frightening as I thought it would be," said Mom. "We should have done it five minutes after Carlin bought the station."

"One minute," said Dad.

"How about syndication?" I asked. "Buzz said something about having contacts."

"He mentioned that to us, too," said Mom. "If it comes our way it will be wonderful. But let's celebrate this nibble tonight. How about going to Luigi's Lair and ordering the best meal on the menu, if we can figure out what it is."

"Luigi's Lair?" I wasn't sure. I had bad memories. Andrea. Her red dress. Her deception. But I said, "Terrific."

I went upstairs to do my homework, but it was hard to concentrate. My parents were happy downstairs. Miserable Mr. Carlin might disappear as a household word. Along with Andrea. Everything was changing.

I went to my bookcase and pulled out Buzz's book. Suddenly I had to know what he had written in it. I hoped it was special. I opened the book to his inscription.

To Dana,
Statistically
(and in every way)
ONE IN A THOUSAND.

Love,
Buzz

I read it over and over. Nobody in that long line could have gotten an autograph as wonderful as mine.

I put on my coat, took the book, and went out for a walk. I didn't want my parents to see me taking a book on a walk. It looked silly. But I just wanted it along.

I headed toward Andrea's house. Consciously, subconsciously, I didn't know. I knew I missed Andrea, but I would get over it. I knew Andrea didn't miss me. I was easy to trade off for a new guy. I was expendable.

When I got near Andrea's house I saw someone coming out of a car parked in her driveway. I recognized Sam Domsky, Jennifer's friend. How had Andrea managed that? I watched Sam go up to Andrea's front door and ring the bell. Then I turned around and started to walk home.

I said good-bye to Andrea in my head. No words, no dramatics, no acknowledgment. We were finished.

I thought about Seymour Finkelstein. I had a sad feeling that I would probably never know if he had been worth all the trouble. He would graduate from high school in two years, probably go on to college, and if I wanted to know anything more about him or his life, I'd have to get lost once again on my way to a nonexistent choir practice. And a friendly middle-aged man at Number Eight might spill some bits and pieces of information about Seymour. But I was past doing things like that.

Seymour might call me anyway, as Andrea had

feared. Maybe we'd go out and I'd discover that he was just one big yawn. But whatever happened or didn't happen, Seymour Finkelstein was slipping away as the main attraction in my life. He'd had a quick rise to the top, he'd stayed there for a while, and now he was on the way down. That's the way it is.

I looked down at Buzz's book in my hand. I'd been thinking lately that I was fifteen and Buzz was twenty-one—that was a real age gap. But when I was nineteen, he'd be only twenty-five, and that would make us about even.

Now I was almost home and I saw my mother standing in the doorway waving to me excitedly.

"Where have you been?" she was shouting. "You've got a long-distance phone call."

I ran up the front stairs. "Mom, is it Buzz?"

"How did you know?"